GIRLS ON TOP

GIRLS ON TOP

EXPLICIT EROTICA FOR WOMEN

EDITED BY
VIOLET BLUE

Published in the United States by
Cleis Press Inc., P.O. Box 14697, San Francisco, California 94114.

Printed in the United States.
Cover design: Scott Idleman
Cover photograph: April/Getty Images
Text design: Frank Wiedemann
Cleis Press logo art: Juana Alicia
First Edition.
10 9 8 7 6 5 4 3 2

"The Central Registry" by Remittance Girl was previously published online in 2006 at the Erotica Readers & Writers Association (www.erotica-readers.com/GD/TC-EF/Central.htm). "High Heels" by Elizabeth Colvin was previously published online in the Good Vibes magazine (goodvibes.com) in 2005.

For Jonathan

Contents

INTRODUCTION: THE SUBTLE AND THE OVERT

It's easy to look at the title of this erotica collection by women, for women and make a simple assumption about the content. You might think it's about ladies in leather and dungeons and whips. Or a typical run-through of BDSM scenes in which women are in charge. While there might be one story like that here, when it comes to sex, being a girl on top is much more rich, complex, arousing, and fun than the first conjured stereotype.

The women who wrote each of these stories are not just talented enough to make the final rounds of judging and edits. The gifted authors here portray sexually rapacious female protagonists whose characters are authentic and as flawed as they are erotically heroic; their conflicts in taking charge of their own sexuality are believable and affecting. They are perverse, hilarious, frustrated, powerful, and sometimes they're on the receiving end and *allow* themselves to get what they want, no matter how hard their inner good girl says no. Every single one emerges satiated, as you will, from a graphic sexual exchange that is empowering, downright nasty, and satisfying to the last letter.

It's just not that simple.

I clearly remember the last time I had a boy tied to my bed. Maybe it's so clear because I took pictures of him, and me, us—with him actually shackled, not tied. I'd shopped for the perfect set of white and black ankle and wrist cuffs, to match his usual style of dress and personal taste. Why? Because in the extremely obvious situations when a girl is on top, it's an act of giving, sometimes an act of love, that includes tenderness and attention to detail to make the boy feel cared for. Even if what you're about to do to him is strip him of every last ounce of his power, and maybe go even farther than that.

Strapped to the bed, fully nude and erect, he looked amazing. It took every ounce of willpower for me not to simply sit astride and ride him to completion: a simple end. But then, why bother with the cuffs? Instead, I turned on my spiked heel and left the room. I know you're not supposed to leave anyone tied up alone, but I wasn't going to be gone for long. In the bathroom, I selected my most poppy red shade of lipstick and applied it carefully, slowly, to keep the pigment under control as much as to give him time to think about his predicament. On my way back to the room I picked up the digital camera.

We smiled at each other and I motioned with the camera, soothing him by saying, "Don't worry. This is not for anyone but me." And it was not entirely true. I surveyed my boy and thought that I could hurt him—apply clips and clamps to his nipples, chest, cock, and balls, and slap them off cruelly with a riding crop, as I'd done with other men before him. I could cane the soles of his feet. I could slather his cock with lube, bind it, and penetrate his ass.

I did do some of those things that night. But the first thing

I did to take power wasn't when I told him to strip. It wasn't when I made him lie on the bed while I buckled him down. Or when I abandoned him. The first thing I did was crawl slowly up his body so he could feel my heat, my skin; smell me. And I kissed his mouth, as slowly and sweetly as I could. I took a photo of the kiss.

Next, I made my way back down his body and took what seemed like forever to kiss his chest in perfect red lip prints. I took a picture. I kissed his cock, his thighs, his leg scars from a potentially fatal motorcycle accident. In another time such an accident would've left him dead or without that leg. I kissed his feet. And in a moment of true tenderness, I took a photo of the lip prints, and myself, at his bound feet. Because sometimes taking power feels just the same as giving it.

He has dominated me many times; he is one of the first and the few. But I seldom feel out of power, as long as I get what I want I feel on top of my power, owning it completely. One evening, I was terribly sad, and he came over to my apartment. I'd never let a lover bind me in ropes; I had a box of rope that had been a gift that went unused. He found the box, and quietly told me to take off my clothes. He tied my hands, my arms, my ankles, my legs; he bound my entire body tight. And then he held me and kissed me. It felt as daring and restorative as the times when he would grab a fistful of my hair and spank me—because he knew it made me feel good; gave me what I wanted, what I needed; and afterward I stood a little stronger, a little taller. Well, at least feeling a little more powerful than before.

Strange, isn't it? The ways we girls find our sexual power. But like I said, this book isn't all ropes and shackles; it's women in ordinary—and sometimes extraordinary—situations, deciding that they are, in fact, the ones on top. Some of the stories are true fiction, cops and robbers stories but too goddamned hot to put down once you start; others are about situations you've been in yourself, the human condition of the girl on top writ large. That's when you just want it so bad, you take it. Or you torture it out of someone—physically, or otherwise. And not all of these stories are heterosexually focused, nor do they play by gender rules all the time—these stories are about girls who break the rules, whether it's their own or society's rules about sex—because they want to get off.

It's an exciting collection. Read it aloud to your lover, and see what happens.

"The Central Registry" by Remittance Girl is the punk of the lot; a pierced party girl decides that enough is enough with the Jehovah's Witnesses that keep interrupting her Saturday hangovers, and she executes a perfect plot to "save" both men at once. In "The Hostage" by B. J. Franklin, we're treated to a night of crime involving bank robbers and a tough, sexually pent-up female security guard who takes on a crime ring, complete with scenes of gay male and group sex where one woman takes all and gets a good deal. S. J. Frost's "Quarterbacking" is a sweet trip into first-time girl-on-top domination, and we get to see a star athlete get his first taste of a strap-on.

Erica K. takes us deep into female fantasies of male domination and forced male cocksucking in the rough but surprisingly loving "Erica's John." When a girl goes out for a night of fun at a mixed orientation bar she finds herself grinding down to business with an androgynous stranger, making "First Time" by Amy Wadhams a truly sexually adventurous tale of takedown.

"Gone Huntin'" by Anusha Ramkissoon-Forte speaks to the impatient girl in all of us who stalks her prey, playing idly, almost bored with her sexual target, much like a cat and its mouse, but with a much more satisfying finish. Rebecca Boyd's "Balzac's Monster" is a slightly more evil story of girl on top, where a girl who could devour her boy if she let herself, but instead maintains a sexual relationship of distance and delicious hands-on cock discipline, making each of his orgasms her property, and hers alone. Taking a more playful approach to girls and taking sexual chances, "High-Speed Wireless" by Miranda Logan is a public sex adventure that only looks like a solo, unless you count the boy daring her ever farther on the other side of her laptop's screen.

Not all tales start out with a girl in the driver's seat; in "Metamorphosis" by Anastasia Mavromatis, the protagonist has long taken the backseat in her life, to both her husband and mother, and finally loses it, transforming herself strikingly and finding her true self on top of, and between the legs of another girl, roughly sixty-nine degrees away from her former life. "New York Peep Show" by Virgie Tovar is all about a girl with huge breasts who loves to see them admired and puts herself into the ultimate position to get what she wants: to be used by her lover and worshipped by unseen breast lovers, all at once. Tamara Rogers takes us back to the dorms for a very unusual quickie in "Philosophy Class," where one phone call leads to dirty talk, mutual masturbation, and an ending with a twist.

She's not unsure about taking charge, she's downright nervous; the girl in "Blue Cock" by Maddy Stuart knows what to do with that cock—give him what he's been asking for—but it takes a bit of turnabout for her to get off on her "little whore" and learn to come inside her harness. Caught off guard by both her attraction to a friend and then his private cross-dressing female sexual identity, the girl in "Spring Fever" by Giselle Renarde discovers how hot this version of lesbianism can be.

Being on top and getting what you want and need isn't always something you can predict and be in charge of—as the cafe counter girl in "The Morning Trade" by Angela Caperton discovers when her fantasies are pushed in front of her face and she rides out a conquering orgasm at someone else's hands (and cock). A story that will stay with you for days, "The Rat-Catcher" by Layla Briar involves an older girl on top who makes a man give her what she needs, perfectly making him think it's his game. Speaking of games, "High Heels" by Elizabeth Colvin is a teasing, taunting game of foot fetish play, where the girl with the hot feet makes an evening out of working her boy into a froth until letting him—letting him—adore her feet until it's orgasms for all.

When lust and desire take control, all bets are off, as seen in "The Woman in His Room" by Saskia Walker where a young woman crushes after a guy so strongly that when he brings another woman back to his room, she breaks the fourth wall of fantasy and reality with a scorching, unexpected encounter. With almost (but not actually) the sound of a whip crack, "With a Smile on Your Face" by Jana Corell is a breakup-sex turn-about in which the previously compliant heroine finally gets the pussy licking she's wanted, and lets the guy know that to keep that smug "friends with benefits" smile on his face he's going to learn about being on his knees—and we know he likes it. Unpredictable, and with a gay male mix for a girl who wants it all (and gets it), "Two Strings to Leon's Bow" by Anais Morten makes me think that when a girl wants, takes, and gets, anything is possible—and the ending feels free, light, and wonderful.

Who knew that being on top could be so dreamy, desirable, layered, compassionate, and downright fierce, all at once?

I hope you'll find this collection as arousing, inspiring, and extraordinary as I do.

Violet Blue
San Francisco

THE HOSTAGE

B. J. Franklin

Last month was the third time that the Followers of Hermes, named after the ancient Greek god of thieves and trickery, succeeded in getting away with a fortune from a high-security bank on the first day of the month without causing any casualties. It could soon be four. We all know what day it is tomorrow—and the police still have no idea how they're doing it."

The newscaster, in her early thirties with short blonde hair and perfect makeup, turned to the man next to her. "I have a hunch the police know more than they're saying, John. What do you think?"

I turned off the television. The police knew no more than the newscaster. I was the only female security guard working for the largest bank in London, and I was worried. The other banks hit had been in New York, Tokyo, and Madrid, and it was only a matter of time until they got to us. My boss was worried too. Every security guard would be on duty tomorrow, and the bank would be closed to all customers and employees.

The other security guards were outwardly unconcerned, but I knew that was just bravado. That day, a grateful but anonymous client had sent our firm four bottles of a very expensive white wine and everyone had had a glass in the evening before leaving. All the big, tough guys who would usually have scorned anything that wasn't beer had downed a full glass in seven seconds flat. I'd accepted the glass but had poured it into the nearest potted plant at the first opportunity.

Bleargh. Give me a nice, cold orange juice any day.

I could understand why they needed to fortify themselves. I was in need as well, but in a different way.

There was a bar of luxury chocolate next to me and my hand was between my thighs. It was running up and down my slit, making my bottom squirm against the cotton sheets and my nightdress ride up around my waist. I needed a good, long wank to release the built-up tension or I would get no sleep at all.

An image filled my mind of two of my work colleagues kissing passionately. Alan is tall and blond and Craig is small and dark, and in my lust-filled mind, they made a beautiful couple. Both my hands were busy, circling my clit and rubbing my nipples until I couldn't wait a moment longer. I used the right pressure on my aching nub and finally let myself come, arching my back and digging my heels into the bed as pleasure streaked down my spine. It took several minutes for the delicious tingles to stop, and I barely had enough energy to turn off the light before falling into a deep and satisfied sleep.

When I arrived at work the next morning, there were so many of us that we were put into threes rather than our customary pairs.

I met Alan and Craig's eyes without blushing. Fantasy and reality are two completely different things—or so I thought. It was only eight o'clock and it wasn't until nine that things got weird.

I needed the bathroom, so I left Alan and Craig at our post halfway down the long corridor to the vault. On my way back, I heard soft moans on my left from the kitchen. Curiosity got the better of me and I peered round the door. My boss had our prim but superefficient secretary bent forward over the flimsy plastic table, her long skirt bunched up around her hips as he thrust inside her repeatedly from behind.

I gaped like an idiot.

My brain refused to accept what my eyes were seeing. It was like coming across an X-rated scene in a Narnia book, or in Harry Potter. Her moans were getting louder as my boss increased the tempo of his thrusts, and I was horrified to feel moisture gathering between my thighs. Their obvious excitement was turning me on.

I slammed the door closed and ran away from the hypnotizing scene, down the corridor toward my partners and sanity.

I heard them before I saw them.

"Craig, no. Stop, please." Alan's voice was deep and husky and held a pleading note I'd never heard from the six-foot-five ex–rugby player before. It was followed by a long, throaty moan that was so filled with sexual desire, my whole body responded. My pulse sped up and my nipples tightened.

My feet led me around the corner. Alan was braced against the wall, his head thrown back and his lips slightly parted. Craig was kneeling in front of him, his hand clamped around the shaft of Alan's straining cock while his tongue danced across the head. No wonder Alan was begging. Craig's free hand was rubbing the bulge at his own groin, and it was clear that soon he would be openly wanking.

It was just like my fantasy. But neither of them had given

any hint of being gay before, never mind being attracted to each other. This was just as wrong as the other pseudo-couple I'd seen.

I cursed myself for feeling obliged to break up such a beautiful sight. "Guys," I said loudly.

They ignored me completely.

I tried again. "Alan! Craig! What the hell are you doing?" No response. That was when the first trickle of fear went down my spine.

There were footsteps behind me. I drew my gun, but just as quickly, I dropped it. There was a machine gun pointed at my head. Scared and horny I might have been, but I was not stupid. Two men wearing black balaclavas were behind the gun. "How cliché," I thought and had the insane urge to giggle.

"Don't you drink?" one of them asked. His voice was soft and surprisingly calm.

I blinked at the seemingly random question. "What?"

"Alcohol. Don't you drink it?"

I frowned, trying to make the connection. "No. I don't like the taste."

They looked at each other. "We've been lucky so far," the same man observed. "There had to be one." He chuckled. "Glad she's so pretty. Plan Stockholm it is."

They moved so swiftly there was nothing I could do. The silent man held my arms pinned behind my back so my breasts thrust forward, my still-hard nipples pressed indecently against my shirt. The talkative man flicked one nipple with his thumb, and I had to suppress a gasp of pleasure as a sharp jolt shot straight to my clit.

The bastard knew exactly what my reaction was. He put his mouth next to my ear. "This is going to be fun," he whispered, and I felt myself cream.

Horrified, I turned my face away. "Craig! Alan!" I screamed, but they were oblivious to anything but each other.

"They can't hear you, darling. That's the point." He picked Alan's shirt up off the floor, where Craig had thrown it in the heat of passion, and bound it tight around my eyes. "You can scream if you like. We won't mind."

They manhandled me—literally, their octopus hands were everywhere—along the corridor and up the stairs. At one point, my hand was lifted into the air and moved up and down purposefully.

"What was that for?"

"You were waving at the security camera. We left one working. Makes it more fun."

I ground my teeth in helpless rage.

They maneuvered me into the back of a vehicle—I could feel the floor thrumming underneath us with the engine—and handcuffed me to some kind of metal bar. The air smelled faintly musty and the metal was cold against my wrists.

I shivered as a door slammed shut. Instinct told me the bossman was still there, with the husky whisper and knowing fingers. We were alone, and god help me, my pussy was soaked. I tried pressing my thighs together but that only made it worse.

Suddenly, soft fingers were on the nape of my neck. The blindfold fell from my eyes and I was gazing at my captor. Eyes so dark they were almost black met mine, and I gasped. I couldn't help it. He was beautiful. Sharp cheekbones, a full and sensuous mouth, and wavy dark hair that just brushed his shoulders.

I wanted him. And I had the perfect excuse. He was the one with the gun.

It was quite dark in the back of the vehicle. There were no windows and just a single, dim light attached to the ceiling, making it seem private and intimate. There was a low table a couple of feet away that was bolted to the floor and had two open bottles of wine on it. I didn't know much about wine, but I recognized the label—the same as the bottles from that anonymous client yesterday.

That was when it clicked.

I glared at the boss, who was standing there patiently, waiting for me to put two and two together and make five. "What the fuck did you put in that wine? You should patent it—it would completely replace Viagra. And it would be a rapist's dream."

He smiled. "The real name for Viagra is Sildenafil and our version isn't dissimilar. It's absorbed slower from the gut so it doesn't have an effect until twelve hours after ingestion, but like Viagra, it requires some underlying attraction—arousal starts in the head, after all. All those people fucking right now are genuinely attracted to each other at some basic level."

I thought of Alan and Craig and my heart leaped with joy. "So why don't the police warn banks not to accept the wine? They could say it knocks people unconscious or affects their memory or something."

"Actually, darling, it does that too. A couple of extra ingredients erase all memories from the past twenty-four hours and make people fall into a deep sleep after an hour or so. Your colleagues at the bank will start feeling very sleepy after their multiple orgasms. The police can't make the connection because it isn't there for them to make. Those two bottles are for me and my men; a celebratory drink after our successful heist."

This long and detailed explanation was making me worried. "Why are you telling me all this?"

He stepped right into my personal space and looked down into my eyes. "Because you won't remember it. Plan Stockholm was prepared in case there was a hot woman for us to play with who hadn't drunk the wine. Stockholm Syndrome is when people fall in love with their captors because they grow dependent on them, but we don't want you in love. Just in lust. You're going to have a drink laced with Memorenafil—that's what we call our concoction. We'll give you something to make you sleep until the drug takes effect, and we'll each visit you after that. You think I'm hot; I can tell."

I felt myself blushing and hoped the darkness hid it. "Sure of yourself, aren't you?"

"I know that look in a woman's eyes. You're horny and we're all attractive." He ran a finger down my cheek, which made my body aware of how much it craved a man's hands. Right at that moment, it didn't care whose hands they were. "You'll be more than happy to fuck us. The others are sexy enough to whet your appetite—though I'll be first in the queue." He rubbed his thumbs over my nipples and felt me shudder. "We'll release you afterward and you won't remember any of it. A terrible shame, really."

"That doesn't make me feel better," I snarled and jerked away. Feeling one of my hands slip out of its cuff, I froze, but luckily, he hadn't noticed. He had moved over to the small table and from behind the bottles, where I couldn't see, he produced a tall, elegant wineglass, a bottle of water, and a small glass vial.

"Since you don't drink, you can take your medicine with water." When the glass was half full, he counted ten drops of the drug into it. The clear water turned a pale gold. He was about to bring it over when there was a loud rap on the door.

Another man in a black balaclava put his head round the door. "Sorry, Boss. We need you for a second."

The bossman put the glass back on the table and walked toward the door. "You can look at it for the next few minutes and think about what's going to happen," he told me cruelly as he pulled his balaclava back on before leaving.

As soon as he was gone, I tried to free myself. The cuffs had not been designed for wrists as small as mine, but the other one remained infuriatingly stuck.

Giving up, I strained the cuff to its limit and discovered I could just reach the glass of water and the bottles of wine on the table. An idea was forming in my mind and I let it simmer for a moment before it crystallized.

I poured the liquid meant for me onto the floor behind the table and half-filled the glass again with water. I tapped a drop of the drug into it. The water stayed clear. It took two more drops for it to turn pale gold and I could only hope the drug wouldn't be effective at less than half the dose.

The vial was still almost full. I added some to each of the open bottles of wine and swirled them around to mix it properly. With the men high on lust, I'd stand a much better chance of escape.

The door handle turned and I moved quickly away from the table, forcing my wrist back into the cuff as the bossman came in, accompanied by five other men. Their balaclavas were on so all I could see were their eyes glowing with anticipation. They put the large bags they were carrying carefully down on the floor and came to stand around me in a loose half circle.

I swallowed. I hated being the center of attention.

"They all wanted to watch," the bossman said. He picked up the glass from the table and brought it over. "Voilà, mademoiselle," he declared and placed it against my lips.

He tipped the glass forward and, out of the corner of my eye, I saw another man caress his gun. I swallowed. There was no point in making a scene.

When the glass was empty, one of the other men stepped forward. He raised his hand and I felt something in my arm, near my shoulder. It hurt and I swore at him, but he just laughed. He stepped back and I saw the needle and now-empty vial in his hand.

I was barely aware of the activity around me as the injection started taking effect. The last thing I remembered was the bossman running his thumb over my nipple, and despite everything, knowing I wanted him to do it again.

It was only gradually I realized I was awake. My arms were heavy but no longer chained to anything. I kept my eyes closed in case anyone was watching and strained to hear a sound, anything that would tell me I was not alone. The only thing I could hear was my own breathing.

I was lying on a soft bed. I could feel the cover beneath me cool against my skin—against my back, my thighs, and the cheeks of my butt. I was completely naked on top of the covers.

I opened my eyes. The room was large and the only light came filtering in through the thick dark curtains, but there was enough to see that the bed was by far the dominant feature of the room. There was a small bedside table and a wardrobe, and that was it. No one was there but me and I savored the privacy while I could.

It didn't last long. I saw movement out of the corner of my eye. The door opened and I had to squint against the unexpected glare of light. A silhouette appeared that slowly resolved into the shape of a man as my eyes became used to the brightness.

"Miss me, darling?" a voice said. It was the sexy bossman. The balaclava was gone and he was wearing a black sleeveless top and black jeans. He came closer to the bed and I could see that the top showed off his well-defined shoulders and biceps.

Their other drug was starting to affect me. A rush of heat was spreading through my veins, making my breasts swell and my pussy throb. "Don't flatter yourself," I said. "I've been looking forward to meeting your gorgeous friends."

Two men were hovering in the doorway. One had an ordinary face but an extraordinary body. He was bare-chested and the smattering of dark hair only emphasized his washboard abs and smooth, tanned skin. The other had a trim, tight body, but that wasn't the first thing even I noticed when I looked at him.

He was beautiful. Young and beautiful—early twenties at the most. He had big, blue eyes with long lashes, but they were just the highlight of a combination of striking elements that all blended into a delicious whole. He saw the way I was looking at him, and to my delight, he blushed. Those lovely eyelashes lowered and he looked down at the floor, a rosy flush over his cheeks. It was my turn to chuckle.

Bossman didn't like my attention focused away from him. He put his hand under my chin and moved my face back in his direction. I met his eyes and realized he had certainly drunk the wine—and it must have been soon after I had for the drug to work so fast. He kissed me passionately, his tongue demanding entry that I was happy to grant. The advance and retreat of his tongue mimicked what I really needed but wasn't enough to satisfy. I knew the other two were watching and that turned me on more. I needed to keep them there until the drug could affect them too.

I moved the bossman's hands so they were cupping my breasts. He groaned and our kiss became even hotter. The drug was affecting his control and I knew it wouldn't be long before he was completely in its grip. His hands moved with such assurance and his body was so firm and strong against mine.

I melted into him and let him explore my nudity, though his hands kept returning to my breasts as if drawn there by magnets. Every time, he lingered a little longer, and my tight, swollen nipples loved his expert caresses. He squeezed them both hard and when my body arched against him, silently begging for more, he fell back onto the bed and drew me down with him.

I was still just able to think. As his hot mouth closed over one nipple, I threw my head back in unfeigned ecstasy but made sure I could see the door.

The two men were staring at me transfixed and their glazed expressions showed they had also drunk the wine. I reached out a hand and they almost ran toward me. I guided the beautiful boy down next to the bossman so his mouth could tease my other nipple.

My body loved that. I was so wet I could feel moisture trickling between my thighs. I remembered what the bossman had said about the drug-induced sleep and knew they needed to come before then. Hell, I wanted to come with them. But there was one man left who seemed about to drag them off me.

There was no way I was letting that happen.

Neither of the other two men was looking at my face, so I smiled at him seductively. It's amazing how much you can convey with a look. I told him without words that all this was just to prepare my body for his and that he was the one I really wanted.

His angry glare was soon replaced by the same glazed expression worn by the others. I beckoned him closer and ran my hands over his chest, enjoying those muscles rippling and flexing under my touch. His eyes closed and his mouth parted as I caressed his abs. I realized his stomach must be a hot spot. I continued to stroke and tease, slipping under his waistband but not going down nearly as far as he wanted me to go.

He was putty in my hands. I had a quick peep at the other two men and knew they'd be happy where they were for a while yet.

I unzipped the trousers of the man in front of me and ran my hand over the shaft of his thick, erect cock before my tongue followed the same path. He grunted and tried to thrust inside my mouth, but I held him firmly in place. I was in control of this.

Soon, he was begging. That sent thrills sparking along my nerves and I decided to let him have his reward. I engulfed him to the root and let the tempo speed up. Within seconds, his breathing was choppy. My tongue drifted across the sensitive head of his cock once more and I added an extra twist to my next stroke. That gave him the final push. He shot his load hard and deep inside my mouth so I swallowed almost before I realized it. His knees gave way and he fell to the floor, leaning back against the bed with his eyes closed.

Damn, I was turned on. The bossman and the beautiful boy were still sucking on my breasts but my clit was aching for attention. I couldn't wait any longer.

I ran my fingers through the bossman's wavy, dark hair, enjoying its silky softness, and pulled his head away from my breast. He was reluctant at first and I could sense the overwhelming lust riding him, demanding more.

I licked the sensitive rim of his ear and felt him shudder. "You're so hard, aren't you?" I whispered, so low that only he could hear. "And I'm so wet. I need you inside me, filling me."

He didn't hesitate. He slid down my body, pausing only to suck my nipple one last time, and plunged fully inside me with one long thrust. It was perfect. I'd had enough buildup and my pussy clamped eagerly around his length.

Beautiful boy could sense the change and raised his head to see where his boss had gone. I looked at that stunning face and knew I wanted him where I could watch him as he climaxed.

I didn't give him time to turn round and see his boss fucking me. I ran my hand down his body and found his fly was already unzipped. One squeeze was all it took to make him completely forget the other man. His world narrowed to his throbbing erection and his body's ever-increasing need to come.

"I'd love to feel this gorgeous cock between my tits," I murmured. "I could come just from watching you shoot all over them."

There was no doubt what he would do. He raised himself into a kneeling position, and I squeezed his biceps in open admiration as he did so. He slid his cock between my breasts, and I pressed them together so they enclosed him in a hot, slick tunnel. He gasped and began thrusting in earnest, back and forth, back and forth. He looked like a beautiful, fallen angel seduced by an evil temptress, helpless to resist the pleasure she offered.

He was close and I knew he would bring me with him, especially when the bossman started flicking my clit as he neared his own orgasm. My body tightened and it was my turn to reach for that elusive peak. Bossman cried out as he filled me with his hot come and the beautiful boy soon followed, his face shining with ecstasy. That was more than enough to drive me over the edge too.

It took less than ten minutes for them to fall asleep afterward. I left them there and, still naked, moved into the hall, which was narrow and had white walls and horrible brown carpet.

I'd only taken a few steps when another man appeared. He was your stereotypical fantasy college teacher, with dark-rimmed glasses, untidy hair, and a massive hard-on that was causing a large bulge in his trousers. He looked exactly like the lead role in some sleazy college porn film.

I love sleazy college porn films.

His eyes widened in recognition when he saw me. "How the fuck did you get me to drink it?" he snarled.

I gave him my most innocent expression. "Drink what?"

"Don't play dumb. I created Memorenafil; I know its effects."

So this was needle-man. I moved toward him, swaying my hips and enjoying the way his eyes zoomed in on my bouncing breasts. I was getting turned on again.

I pressed my body against his and began to play with his collar. "I put it in your wine," I purred. "It seemed…appropriate."

He wasn't touching me. Yet. But his voice was husky. "But I had mine with Mike and Jon, after the others drank theirs in the van. Why aren't Mike and Jon here too, desperate to fuck you?"

I made a mental note that I needed to look for them and told the truth. "I don't know." I trailed kisses down his neck. "But since they're not, you have me all to yourself. What are you going to do with me?"

"If you think you're going to seduce me into letting you escape, you can think again," he growled, but the statement lost some of its impact when his hands were caressing my ass.

I nestled into his touch. "How can I escape if I'm with you?" I felt his grip on my buttocks tighten. My lips were only an inch below his.

"Kiss me," I breathed.

His Adam's apple bobbed up and down as he swallowed, trying to resist the effects of his own poison. "I'm not going to let you escape," he repeated as his lips came closer. They covered mine and his control seemed to shatter all at once. He lifted me so his covered erection was pressing up and into my pussy at the perfect angle.

I rubbed my clit over the denim seam and whimpered with arousal. "I'm not going anywhere," I promised, and ground myself repeatedly against him.

He was far too horny to reply. He didn't even try to stop me when my hands attacked his belt buckle. I loosened his belt, unzipped his jeans, and guided him directly inside me. It was so erotic with him fully clothed while I was naked. He had been battling his lust for a while, and I knew he wouldn't last long. I clenched my inner muscles around him just right, tightening and releasing in time with his movements, and he came hard in seconds.

He lay down with his head in my lap and I stroked his hair. He yawned and looked only a little embarrassed afterward. I carried on lulling him into total relaxation and felt his resistance weakening.

"Sleep," I whispered. "There's no need to fight it."

"You'll run away." I could tell how much even those few words cost him.

"No, I won't. You owe me an orgasm."

He chuckled and I felt him fully relax at last. I stayed there for another minute and then eased my body out from under his. Something told me he would enjoy pleasuring a woman.

I went carefully down the stairs, listening for the mysterious Mike or Jon.

I almost tripped over them. They were sixty-nining in the middle of the downstairs hall. It was like with Alan and Craig, except these two were further along. Their mouths were working hard and their hands were cupping each other's balls or teasing a tight, puckered asshole. They were far too engrossed in their mutual enjoyment to notice anyone, least of all a naked woman.

One of the most difficult things I've ever done was leaving them there.

I stepped over them and went to find a phone. I finally succeeded in the kitchen. Not sure what else to do, I dialed the number the police had set up for anyone with information about the bank thieves. It was supposed to work from any country in the world.

"Hello," the operator said in a bored voice. "Followers of Hermes information line." He was probably fed up with dealing with prank calls.

I didn't bother with chitchat. I said, "My name is Karen Lawson, and I was kidnapped from the Royal Bank this morning by the Followers of Hermes. I'm in their headquarters. If you trace this call, you can find me—and them."

There was silence on the other end as he struggled to adjust to this startling news. I was quickly passed on to someone senior. He asked me if I could see a street sign or anything outside to indicate where in the world I might be. I peered out of a small window and saw, of all things, the Eiffel Tower standing straight and tall a few miles away. I recognized it from postcards.

"I can't see anything," I told him.

"Then it will take us a while to track you," he warned. "Is there somewhere safe you can hide?"

I thought of Mike and Jon enjoying themselves in the hall nearby, and the tips I might pick up to share with Alan and Craig when I seduced them after I got back to London. I thought of the pornographic college teacher asleep upstairs who owed me an orgasm.

"Oh, yes," I assured him. "There's no rush."

QUARTERBACKING

S. J. Frost

Her heart pounding with nervous anticipation, Hannah glanced at the clock and saw that not a full minute had passed since she'd last checked. She let out a sigh of frustration, as much at the slow passage of time as at her own impatience. Deciding she needed to take her mind off waiting, she glanced around the bedroom to make sure she had everything laid out how she wanted.

Already tied to the wooden posts of the headboard were four strips of dark purple silk: two short ones with padded Velcro cuffs at the ends; two longer ones, each with a black leather strap, adjustable by the steel buckle and steel rimmed holes tied to them. On the nightstand sat a dildo and a vibrator. The dildo mimicked a true flesh cock complete with balls at the end, and she'd chosen it for its modest size: slender, with a shaft of roughly four inches. The vibrator was a simple black plastic rod with ridges. Beside those sat a new bottle of lube.

Satisfied, she went to the full-length mirror on the back of the door to the master bathroom and assessed herself. Her body was squeezed into a corset of black lace, her B-cup breasts were pushed up in two mounds of thick cleavage, and she had to admit, she wore the corset well. Even though lingerie had never been her thing, she figured if Collin held true to his statement about allowing her to do with him what she would, the least she could do was give him something he'd enjoy looking at.

She pulled her black silk thigh-highs up and adjusted one of the straps connecting them to the corset. She turned, checking out her ass in the thong, frowning at the hint of cellulite that dimpled her cheeks. Though she worked out three times a week, nature had its ways of reminding her that she had crested the thirty-year mark two years previously. She flipped her hand at the mirror. It didn't matter. She was long past the point of worrying about what men thought of her ass. If they liked it, great. If not, their loss.

She pulled some of her dark brunette hair over her shoulders, letting the silken strands curl over her cleavage to rest in the groove of her breasts. She met her own light brown eyes and smiled. Tonight she would finally get to live out one of her fantasies. Hopefully. Providing that Collin didn't chicken out, or maybe even herself. She pushed the latter thought away. No, she might be nervous, but there was no way she was going to back out of this.

Part of her still wondered if her desires were normal. Was it right for a woman to want to dominate a man? For herself, she felt she was still far from reaching the upper-level domination, as in commanding Collin to be her slave boy and punishing him with whips and wax, and she didn't think this first step would bring her any closer, but for once in her life she wanted to have a man at her mercy. She wanted full control. She wanted to play with him, probe him, tease him, torment him.

Hannah laughed softly to herself. Maybe she was closer to that upper level than she thought. Yet for all her sexual life, she had suppressed her feelings, believing them to be wrong, unnatural. Her late teenage years had been spent trying to figure sex out. When she left rural Illinois for Purdue University on a track scholarship, her life at college brought more adventures in intimacy, but also Dan in her sophomore year. They were living together by their junior year, married after graduating, and she loved him and accepted him for all his flaws, both as a person and as a lover as he tended to be a bit boring in both respects.

When her career as a sports reporter finally began to take off, her success sparked resentment rather than pride in Dan. He disliked her traveling, complained about her long hours on the computer writing articles, and accused her of being attracted to every man she interviewed. Their relationship dissolved into more arguments than sex. When it had reached the point of complete misery for them both, they came to the conclusion that happiness might well be waiting for each of them elsewhere, and at the age of twenty-seven, she found herself a single woman once again.

The day her divorce became final she vowed never to marry again, and for three years she enjoyed dating and experiencing different men…for the most part. Despite their varied personalities, so often they were similar in the bedroom—with their male posturing, and the conviction of each that his cock was the finest piece of flesh she would ever have the privilege of taking into her body, when more often than not, it was a letdown.

That all changed after she met Collin. Drafted into the NFL in the first round by the Chicago Bears to be a backup and future replacement for their aging quarterback, Collin's illustrious college career had warranted an interview as he embarked upon his professional one. At twenty-three-years-old, he looked painfully young when she interviewed him, and despite her thoughts of what the handsome young man with his amazing physique, thick dark brown hair, and light green eyes could want with a woman seven years his senior, Collin's flirtatiousness made it clear that he knew very well what he wanted. That same night, she broke her personal rule of never dating athletes.

With him, she discovered how exciting sex could be. Passionate and bold, nothing was too taboo for him. Public places, anal sex with him on top, toys, porn with all sexualities, he seemed game for anything, and could flaunt his masculinity and prowess deservingly, though he never did.

Yet despite their sexual escapades, she realized she was still holding herself back from expressing all that she desired from him. When he proposed to her a month ago, she'd accepted ecstatically, but since that time, she'd come to the decision that she couldn't enter another marriage without knowing if Collin would be willing to surrender to her in the way she wanted him to.

She broached the subject to him that morning, simply asking, "Collin, would you let me do anything I wanted to you?"

Collin laughed, nearly dribbling milk from the mouthful of cereal he'd just taken. "Yeah, babe, I'd let you do anything you wanted to me."

"Even if it's something you're not sure you'd like, or that you're not comfortable with at first?"

He gave her his wicked smirk that always managed to increase her heart rate. "There's nothing you could do to me that I wouldn't like, and so long as it's you doing it, I'd be comfortable with it."

The memory fading, Hannah looked to the bed. She hoped he wouldn't regret those words.

From downstairs, she heard the door to their condo open

and close, followed by Collin's deep voice yelling, "I'm home! Where are you?"

"Upstairs!" she called back, and darted for the bed.

At the sound of his footsteps springing up the hardwood stairs two at a time, she quickly smoothed her hair, crossed her legs, and leaned back on both arms, pushing her chest out. An instant later, Collin appeared in the doorway, a large smile on his face, his height and thick build filling the open space. His dark hair still looked damp from showering after practice, the clean scent of soap and spicy cologne drifted off his skin. His eyes fell on her and widened.

"Oh, my god," he said, his surprise eliciting a couple of soft chuckles. "You look amazing."

"Thanks," Hannah said, meeting his gaze with a soft smile on her lips.

His eyes lifted from hers to the bondage straps on the headboard. They moved next to the nightstand; the dildo, vibrator, and lube.

Hannah watched the realization come over his face. "You're remembering our conversation this morning, aren't you?"

Collin continued to stare at the toys. "Those aren't for me... are they?"

"You said you'd let me do anything."

Collin chuckled again, the sound holding more nervousness than before. "Yeah, I guess I did."

"If you don't want to—"

"No." His smile brightened with his usual playfulness. "Let's give it a shot."

Deciding to grant him one more opportunity to escape, Hannah said, "Only if you're sure."

Collin waved his hand at her. "Woman, I can handle whatever you dish out."

Hannah's smile took on a more malicious edge. "You think so?"

Collin stepped into the bedroom and lifted his voice to a pleading tone. "Just be gentle. I'm delicate."

Through her soft laugh, Hannah said with thick sarcasm, "Yeah, I know how fragile you are."

She stood and wrapped her arms around his waist. Still smiling, Collin bent his head, covering her lips with his own. She pulled his tongue into her mouth, her head moving against his as she sucked and massaged it. Collin groaned deep in his throat and moved his hips closer to her. Through his jeans, Hannah felt his firm cock against her stomach. She slid one hand between them and pressed her palm to it. He pushed his hips harder into her hand.

Hannah slid her hands under his shirt and began lifting it higher, revealing his abdomen lined with hard muscle, his thick pectorals covered in sparse dark hair. Collin gripped his shirt and pulled it the rest of the way over his head as she struggled to do so with her shorter height. Dropping his shirt to the floor, he moved his hands to her back and undid the first hook of her corset.

Hannah reached back, taking his hands in hers. "My clothes stay on. Now be a good boy and fasten that hook again."

Collin's eyebrows raised in surprise. "Yes, ma'am," he said, securing her corset. "What other orders do you have for me?"

Hannah grabbed the top of his jeans, and giving him a sharp jerk forward, freed the button, then moved her fingers to the zipper. "First, you're going to get naked. Then, you're going to lie on your back in the center of the bed. From there, I'll give you my orders as I see the need to."

Collin bowed his head to be closer to her height. "You've always been demanding, making me work hard every time we have sex, but I'm starting to really like this."

"I'm glad, since this is just an introduction. I had so many ideas of things I wanted to do to you, I couldn't figure out where to begin. If we have fun tonight, just think of all the new things we can try. Now take your pants off and do what I told you."

Doing as he was commanded, Collin removed his jeans, black boxer-briefs, and socks, and headed to the bed. He climbed on, moved to the center, and went down on his back. Hannah stalked toward the left side of the bed, her strides slow as she appreciated his supine form. His cock, filled and flushed with eagerness, reared eight inches up from his body. Unlike many men she'd known, Collin kept himself well groomed in his nether regions. Rather than let his pubic hair run wild, he neatly trimmed the dark curls and shaved his sac for the added sensitivity he gained at the soft feel of a tongue coursing along the delicate skin.

Hannah placed one knee on the edge of the bed and reached toward him, drawing her hand down his chest. "You don't look nervous anymore."

"I'm not. I'm curious and excited now."

She brushed her thumb over his left nipple, feeling it perk up under her touch. "If at any point you feel uncomfortable or if I hurt you, just tell me to stop and I will."

Collin smirked up at her. "I wasn't uncomfortable until you said 'hurt.'"

Hannah gave him a disapproving look. "Collin, I mean it."

He laid his hand over hers. "I know, but I'm not worried about it. I trust you."

His words reminded her once again why she had fallen so deeply in love with him. She gave him a single nod and took his left wrist in her hand, stretching his arm over his head. She pulled the shorter of the two silk strips on the left side of the bed forward, tore apart the Velcro and wrapped the cuff around his wrist, being careful to not have it too tight to be comfortable, but tight enough that he knew he was restrained. She crawled onto the bed and moved over him to get to his right side, letting him get a full view of her full cleavage. She took the next short strap and secured his right arm in the same fashion.

Hannah looked down at him to see how he was handling things so far. The large vein in his neck pulsed, betraying his quick heartbeat. She bent over him, claiming his mouth in a long, deep kiss before continuing. She slid off the bed on the left side and tapped his left knee. "Bend your leg back."

Collin hesitated, then did as she asked.

Hannah pressed his knee closer to his shoulder and reached for the longer strip of silk. Picking up the black leather strap on the end, she wrapped it around his thigh near the crook of his knee and buckled it so that his leg was forced to stay bent back. With his left leg secured, she walked around the foot of the bed and did the same with the right. She stepped back to take in her handiwork. Seeing his large, powerful body bound and submissive sent her heart beating in a frantic pace. She'd been damp between her legs at the start, now the silk of her thong felt fully drenched.

Hannah noticed the crimson flush lighting Collin's cheeks. "Are you doing okay?"

"Yeah, it's just I wish you would've picked another color besides purple for these things. It's so girly. Couldn't you have gotten black or camouflage?"

Hannah laughed softly. "I'm sorry, sweetheart. Camouflage wasn't one of the color options. I could've gotten pink."

"Then I guess this isn't that bad," he mumbled.

Hannah stepped up to the bed and touched his cheek with the backs of her fingers. "Other than not liking the color, is everything else okay?"

"If you're asking how I like having my asscheeks pulled

apart and feeling every little breeze on my hole, I'm doing okay with it."

"That's good. Now we can get started."

Collin's tongue flicked out to moisten his lips, his eyes following her as she moved toward the nightstand.

Grabbing the lube and the dildo, Hannah turned back to the bed and climbed on, situating herself between his raised legs. She ran her hand up his hard cock. "I'll start really slow."

His eyes watching her, he managed a slight nod.

Hannah drew her hand back down his length, brushing her fingertips lightly over his heavy sac. She gently squeezed and fondled it, evoking a deep groan from him. She lifted it and held it up while with her other hand she tickled the strip of skin between it and his hole. Collin took in a trembling breath. She moved her gaze to his face, seeing his eyes were closed, his brow creased as he concentrated on the new sensations he was experiencing.

Hannah brought her gaze back to her fingers. She stared down at his pink hole. She realized that this was the first time in her life that she'd ever had the opportunity to fully study a man. She'd seen her share of naked men and the wide array of their packages in their diverse shapes and sizes, but she'd never had a man so bared before her that she could study how his sac hung and shifted, how his cock twitched when she did something he especially liked, the shape and lines around his anus. It all enraptured her, and to have every part laid in wanton offering before her amazed her all the more.

She drew the tip of her middle finger lower and touched his hole for the first time. She saw the muscles clench, then release in involuntary reaction. She circled the perimeter gently, as much familiarizing herself with how it felt as letting Collin become acquainted with her touch. She raised her middle finger to her mouth and coated the tip in saliva. She touched it to him again, and he groaned in response, his hips rolling the slightest bit.

Hannah moved her left hand to his cock and took the shaft in a firm grip. A louder moan rumbled from Collin's throat as she began to slowly pump him while massaging his hole. She noticed his breathing had deepened and quickened.

"Does it feel good?" she asked.

"Y-yeah," Collin said, swallowing hard. "Really good."

Hannah took the lube and dripped some onto her middle finger. She returned her touch to both his cock and his anus, and continued her motions as before. After a long moment, she said, "I'm going to start inserting my finger."

His voice lost, Collin nodded.

Hannah pressed the tip of her middle finger to his hole and pushed inside him. Collin let out a short gasp. She stopped at her first knuckle, rotated her finger inside him around his rim, then withdrew from him, massaging him on the outside as before. She repeated the process, gradually working her finger deeper and deeper into him until she had it buried inside him up to her hand.

She gazed down at her hand, amazement hitting her once again that she was inside a man. The intimacy of it and Collin's trust in her overwhelmed her with emotions of love and tenderness for him, and seeing that he was gaining pleasure from it, pleasure that she controlled, made her feel satisfied and powerful.

She began moving her hand in small thrusting motions, rubbing the soft wet flesh of his channel, feeling the tightness of him slowly slacken. Exhaling a hushed moan, Collin rocked his hips toward her hand. She pulled her middle finger out of him, aligned her index finger with it and dribbled more lube over them, filling the groove of her fingers. She reentered him with both, going up to her middle knuckles. Collin let out a hard groan.

Hannah stopped, her fingers still inside him. "Is it too much?"

Collin shook his head. "No, it's good." A smile curved his lips. "I'm just glad you've got little fingers."

Laughing under her breath, Hannah focused her actions. She stroked his cock to add to his pleasure. She felt his body accepting her, and she pushed deep, crooking her fingers upward to seek out his prostate. Collin gasped loudly, his body flinched, and she knew she'd found the right spot. With tender care, she massaged around the gland. Collin's breathing became quick and ragged, fluid leaked from his slit to his stomach. His groans turned louder, and he rocked his hips as much as he could in his restraints.

Sensing he wasn't going to last if she continued her sensual assault, Hannah eased the pressure on his prostate and pulled her fingers out of him. She grinned at his whimper of protest, then coating her index, middle, and ring fingers thick with lube, she pushed all three in. A high pitched moan came from him. She glanced up to him to see his head was turned to the left, his eyes squeezed shut, his cheek pressed against his thick bicep stretched above his head. She looked back down to his hole that before had been so small and tight, now stretched around her fingers, encasing her in his warm body.

Hannah flicked her gaze to the dildo. She felt he was ready, but wanted to make sure he felt the same. "Do you want to go a little further?"

Collin's head moved in a short nod. "Yeah. Put it in."

Hannah removed her touch from him and took hold of the dildo. She slathered it in lube and applied more around his anus. She put the tip to his entrance and coaxed the flared head inside and over his rim. His muscles tightened. Raising her eyes to him, she saw his jaw visibly clenched, the cords of tendons raised in his neck, his hands balled into fists, and the muscles in his arms straining as he pulled against his bonds.

"Does it hurt?" she asked.

Collin allowed himself a few deep breaths before answering. "No. It feels too damn good. That's the problem."

Hannah smiled. "That's a good problem."

"It's a fucking awesome one," he choked out.

Hannah brought her attention back to the dildo. Steadily, she inched it deeper into him. Where before it had been intimate and emotional when she had her fingers inside him, watching his body take in the fake cock was just simply hot. She shifted on the bed, the small movement causing her saturated thong to press against her swollen clit. She reached down and touched herself, her body responding instantly with a gush of heat in her groin. Too much longer and she wouldn't be able to hold out taking her pleasure from him.

She pushed the dildo in until it was buried up to its plastic balls. Setting a steady rhythm, she began thrusting it in and out of him. She gripped his cock again and pumped him in harmony with her thrusting. Collin rocked toward her, his movements faster than hers in an attempt to drive himself to climax. She considered ordering him to stop, but she felt pity after looking at his face, his expression filled with desperate need, and she decided against it. This was only their first time experimenting like this and with the way things had gone so far, they'd be venturing down this erotic path again. There'd be plenty of time in later sessions to make him hold out.

Hannah pushed the dildo deep inside him, then released it. At her sudden halting of attention, Collin's eyes fluttered open searching for her. Hannah reached up and unbuckled the leather strap holding Collin's left leg back. She guided it for him to relax it down, then freed his right leg and grabbed two pillows.

"Raise your hips," she said.

Collin obliged quickly.

Hannah slid the two pillows under his lower back to keep his ass propped off the bed. With efficient fingers, she unfastened the straps to her thigh-highs, took hold of her thong and wiggled it off. She crawled along his side, her eyes locked on his. She swung her left leg over him and straddled his waist. Lowering her head to his chest, she licked his right nipple, circling and teasing it, tasting the salt of the light sweat he'd formed. She gently plucked it with her front teeth, causing him to take in a hissing breath. She licked a line across his chest to his other nipple, covered it with her mouth and sucked.

Collin groaned her name.

Hannah straightened and stretched for the nightstand, retrieving the vibrator. She slid down his body, smearing his abdomen with her juices. His cock bumped against her ass, and she raised herself up. Reaching down, she took his shaft and squeezed, savoring how the hard flesh didn't yield to her grip. On her knees above it, she positioned it against her slick folds and lowered her body onto the broad head. Once it breached her inside, she dropped down hard and fast. Collin let out a groan closer to a shout; Hannah expelled a choked moan. After experiencing his body from the inside, his presence in her sent her mind floating with ecstasy.

She stretched back and found the dildo had slid half out of him. She pushed it deeper, thrusting it while she raised and lowered herself on his cock. With each exhale, Collin groaned. His legs now free, he braced his feet on the bed and jerked his hips up to meet her.

Hannah shoved the dildo into him, let it go, and grabbed the vibrator. She switched it on and pressed it to her clit. For an instant, she froze, her body going rigid at the shock of pleasure.

She noticed her breathing now matched Collin's frantic pace. Her teasing of him had brought them both to a frenzied state. Pinning the vibrator to her clit, she placed her other hand on Collin's chest and thrust her hips down to his body, riding him with such force he couldn't raise his own to her.

She felt his muscles constrict. Sharp ecstasy sparked through her clit, telling her she was seconds away. She increased her pace still more, the heat building and swirling between her legs. Her muscles clenched Collin's cock, and her orgasm hit. She let out a loud cry, and for a few sweet seconds, nothing existed but physical sensation. As reality returned, she heard Collin's yell of passion, and his cock throbbed as it emptied inside her.

She watched him climax, his mouth opened in panting breaths, wires of muscles straining. He came down from it slowly and lay beneath her fighting for his breath, his arms hanging limp in his restraints, entirely spent. She knew it had been one of his most powerful orgasms and couldn't help but feel pride and joy that she'd been the one to give it to him.

The vibrator hummed on the bed where she'd tossed it during her climax, and Hannah reached to turn it off. She stretched back and found the dildo still inside him. She drew it slowly from him, Collin breathing a soft whimper as it left his body. She raised herself and eased his softening cock from her, then tugged the Velcro cuffs free of his wrists. His arms dropped to the bed with a heavy thump. Hannah moved to his side and lay down, curling against his body, draping her arm and leg over him.

"I hope you liked everything I did," she said.

"I'm not sure," he said, his voice husky from exertion. "I think we should try it again in a little while so I can decide."

"Have I opened a new door for us?"

Collin rolled his head toward her, burying his smiling lips in her hair. "You blasted it open."

She sat up and looked into his eyes. "You don't know how much it means to me that you trust me so much you're willing to do things like this for me."

"Well, it's not like I get nothing out of it," he laughed.

She smiled at him and combed her fingers through his damp hair. "I love you."

Collin put his hand on the back of her head, entwining his fingers in her hair. "I love you, too."

Hannah placed a light kiss on his lips. She laid her head back on his shoulder, confident and excited about their future together.

CENTRAL REGISTRY

Remittance Girl

Due to the previous night's overindulgence I couldn't make a proper fist. That was why I was lowering my face over the coffee mug that sat steaming on the kitchen table, carefully attempting to make lip contact with the ceramic rim. Then the doorbell rang.

"Motherfucker." The brew was scalding. The bell was cruel.

I took a slurp of coffee, then another, and let its bitterness slither down my throat, taking the aspirin on my tongue with it. It was only a matter of time, I promised myself, before the combination of painkillers and caffeine kicked in. Then I wouldn't be wishing for death anymore.

The dumb, miniature replica of Big Ben sounded again. Ignoring it, I bowed low before the coffee god and sucked. Just a couple more minutes and life would be good again.

The bell rang a third time. I moaned and shifted off the dinette chair. Whoever it was, they weren't going away. There were only two ways to stop the torture: one was to rip out the electrical wires that snaked their way to the bell's button and the other was to answer the door. I weighed my present inclination for destruction against my inability to make a fist, then shuffled down the hallway and opened the door.

"What?"

"Excuse me, ma'am. It's a fine morning, and we're just wondering if we could take a moment of your time. We're from the Church of—" There were two of them, dressed like the Bobbsey Twins in white shirts, flannel trousers, and burgundy ties.

"Jesus fucking Christ!"

"...Jehovah's Witnesses."

"You've got to be joking!" I moaned. It's not like I hadn't sent enough of these idiots away from my door; you'd think they'd be smart enough to pool their resources and have a central registry somewhere with a list of houses that just weren't buying.

The duo looked too damn preppy to live. It there was any justice in the world they'd both get malignant melanoma.

"Oh, it's no joke, ma'am. We have extremely good news for you." The one doing the talking was nauseatingly focused, but his silent partner was staring at my toes.

I pushed the mass of blue-black, teased-to-death hair out of my face so they could see me glower, and get a good look at my eyebrow piercing. "Do I look remotely like someone who wants your fucking good news, asshole?"

"God wants all his children to hear the good news, ma'am."

The coffee was kicking in, or maybe it was the aspirin hitting my bloodstream, but I could feel the rage rising in my throat. "What kind of sadists are you, anyway, ringing doorbells at nine o'clock on a Saturday morning? Get the fuck off my doorstep before I puke on you."

That seemed to do the trick. The talker apologized, turned,

and started to walk back down the stone path. The other one seemed to be stuck; he was still staring at my feet.

"Do you want to lick them?"

He spun and fled, catching up with his buddy at the side-walk.

Usually, I'm not a vengeful person and, ask anyone, I seldom hold a grudge. But the incident with the sanctimonious pricks of Kingdom Hall wormed its way under my skin and started to fester. It was blatantly uncivilized, I thought, to brandish fire and brimstone at someone the morning after she's had a night of partying.

I crawled back into bed, hoping to return to painless oblivion, but the anger had my adrenalin pumping. I tossed and turned a bit, trying to get into a snuggly, sleep-friendly position, to no avail. Frustrated, I pulled my oversized T-shirt off, wriggled out of my panties, and settled on a long, soothing wank.

At first I wasn't really thinking of anything. I went through my usual routine of lying on my back with my legs spread, teasing the tip of my middle finger around the outside of my hooded clit. (I have one of those barely hooded ones, so I have to start off gently.)

Once I could feel my juices flowing, I began to take long, slow strokes through the valley of my inner labia, spreading the slipperiness around. That's when I started to fantasize, and how I evolved my plan.

By the time I'd brought myself close to orgasm, the scenario was intricately detailed and developed and all the contingencies were accounted for. I plunged two fingers deep into my cunt and groaned as the muscles convulsed around them.

If those two little fuckers ever rang my doorbell again, vengeance would be mine.

* * *

Not a day went by without me masturbating my way to further elaborations of my sick little plan. By the following Friday, my fantasy had developed a life of its own and turned rather obsessive; so much so that, while out clubbing on Friday night, I purposefully moderated my alcohol intake. I wanted to be bright-eyed and bushy-tailed the next morning.

And that's how I woke up—at 8:00 A.M., no less.

I had a shower, pulled my hair back into some semblance of normality, changed my eyebrow barbell for a tiny, demure silver ring, and applied as little eyeliner as it was possible to use without triggering withdrawal symptoms. I crowned the effect with a coat of five-year-old taupe lipstick, which I found at the back of the bathroom cabinet. I looked at myself in the mirror and almost fainted.

Fuck, did I ever look nice.

Finding the right clothes wasn't easy. I had to rummage through an old suitcase for something appropriate: a floral print dress I'd worn only once, to my aunt's second wedding. I tried it on without a bra, but it looked odd, so I compromised and went for nipple-less black net. The matching panties, however, I declined, along with any footwear.

I sat at the kitchen table, looking like Mary Ann, from "Gilligan's Island" (well, sort of), sipping coffee and watching the clock.

At ten past nine, I started to worry that they weren't going to show. Perhaps I'd been just a little too forceful the week before. Maybe, somewhere, there actually was a central registry. One by one, all my beautifully crafted plans started curling at the edges, and only when I was seriously considering rolling myself a cheer-up joint did the bell ring.

* * *

I flung the door open and smiled pleasantly. As a consequence of the weather having warmed a little, they had traded their gray flannel trousers for chinos, and caution, it seemed, had been thrown to the wind; both of them had their shirtsleeves neatly rolled up.

"Good morning, ma'am. It's a lovely day and we're just wondering if we could take a moment of your time. We're from Kingdom—"

"Yes. We met last week, remember?"

"—Hall, and have come to bring you some good—"

"Snarling bitch? Ring any bells?"

They glanced nervously at each other. I'd obviously put them off their stride. The smaller, quiet one looked down at my feet again. He was my favorite.

The talker swallowed hard, adjusted the fake smile, and looked me in the eye. "People aren't always ready to hear the good news, ma'am." He was a little taller than his buddy, a bit thicker-set and a fairer-skinned. Frankly, he looked like a jock—not my type, really.

"So true," I gushed. "But I've given what you said last week some thought, and I think I'm ready to hear the good news now. Would you like to come in?" I smiled back, showing teeth.

The jock's jaw fell slack, and he elbowed the little cutie. I stepped aside and pulled the door open wider. "Please, come sit down and have a juice or something. At least give me the opportunity to apologize for last week. Then, maybe, you can explain how all this saving stuff works."

They obviously had some sort of secret signals, because something passed between them and the jock nodded. "That would be wonderful, ma'am, if you have the time."

"Oh, I think the time is probably nigh," I muttered, leading them into my living room.

At that point, I did wonder whether they weren't going to balk. I had forgotten that my interior décor wasn't all that conducive to revelation. For one thing, I have a massive Marilyn Manson poster from his *Antichrist Superstar* tour on the wall. Then, there was the bookshelf full of voodoo-Barbies I'd acquired diligently over the years. My favorite was the Malibu Barbie with the head cleaved in two with a razor blade, naked but for a miniature dog collar.

"See?" My hand swept over the room. "I really do need saving in the worst way. Can I get you some apple juice?"

They both refused politely and sat down: the jock on the couch, and the quiet one in my battered armchair. They gave each other nervous looks.

"I'm Candice, by the way." I walked up to the armchair and held out my hand. The quiet one shook it and mumbled, "John."

"As in 'the Baptist'? Too cool! I promise not to do any dancing with seven veils." I guess it went over his head because he just grinned.

The jock stood as I offered him my hand. "I'm Brian," he said, and reseated himself.

"Nice to meet you both." I knelt down on the carpet about midway between them, folded my hands in my lap, and looked at each of them expectantly. "So, where do we start?"

"Well, first of all, you have to accept Jesus into your heart," said the jock.

I smiled. "Brian, I'll be happy to accept Jesus anywhere you want to put him."

He gave me a little nod and continued. "Then, of course, you have to acknowledge that you're a sinner, in need of redemption, as we all are, Candice."

"Oh, that's easy. I'm a huge sinner. Heaps of sin. I'm just

drippin' with it." I looked over at John the Baptist. "But I can hardly believe you're a sinner, John. You don't look like you've committed a sin in your entire life!"

He perked up a little. "Oh, but I am. We all are! But God loves us anyway. Isn't that wonderful?"

I slid my eyelids half shut. "It is, John! It certainly is. Because you have no idea what dark, hot, wet, thoroughly disgusting sins I've committed."

I switched my attention over to Brian. "Would you like to know, Brian?" Moving closer to where he was sitting, I balanced my crossed arms on his knees and perched my chin on top of them. "Should I confess them to you?" I felt his legs go rigid.

"N-no. We're not Catholic, Candice. We don't have that kind of confession. God, our father, knows all your sins already."

"Really?" I slowly began to pull his knees apart and move between them. "I'm not convinced that God-the-Father could forgive them, Brian. I've done some really terrible things. Awful, carnal stuff—sins of the flesh, you know? Sometimes with other people, sometimes just by myself. Coveting my neighbor's wife and his ass and generally worshipping a lot of false idols, taking the Lord's name in vain when I come really hard. Stuff like that."

I have to admit I felt a certain flush of pride and vindication as I spotted a definite bulge in his crotch. I looked up into his face and then down at his hard-on, making quite sure he saw me do it. Then, I licked my lips slowly.

"And Brian?"

"Yes?" His response was little more than a whisper.

"I'm not so sure I can stop committing them. They're awful fun and..." I gripped the zipper on his chinos between my thumb and forefinger, "they feel so damn good."

I heard a quick intake of breath as I eased his fly down. By the time I popped the press-stud on his pants and pulled the sides apart to reveal a blindingly white pair of boxers, he wasn't breathing at all. I reached through the breach and pulled out a throbbing cock. "Temptation is a terrible thing, Brian. It's so hard to resist."

My fingers curled around the thick, veiny cock in my hand and stroked it. Meanwhile, I glanced over at John the Baptist to see how he was taking all this. He looked like someone had strapped him to the chair and stapled his eyes open.

"Don't you find sin hard to resist, John?" I eyed him while I grazed his buddy's cock with my lips. "Well?"

"It's...it's...very hard," John stuttered back.

"I'll bet it is," I whispered, before engulfing Brian's cockhead with my mouth.

I don't mind saying that I gave him much better than he deserved. At first he just sat there and made little whiny noises, but after a while I guess you could say that the spirit moved him, or at least his hips. Before long, I had a full-blown moaner on my hands.

It never occurred to me that irony could get me wet, but apparently it does.

"Oh, sweet Jesus!" he yelled, pumping his cock upward.

I did consider submitting to a little laying on of hands, but I didn't want Brian to lose it down my throat and then get all remorseful, so I stopped.

I gave him a big grin as I pulled off him. "Still in the grip of temptation, Brian?"

He nodded, panting.

"I need you to hold that thought while I find out if John here is as prone to sinning as the rest of us. I bet you'd like to know too, huh?" He nodded again, eyes glazed.

I did actually feel a little sorry for John the Baptist, as I walked over to him, unbuttoning the top of my dress. He looked scared.

"John? Are you a big bad sinner?" I cooed.

He wasn't paying attention. His eyes were glued to my tits. I straddled him on the chair and heard him groan. "Mmm, I think you are."

I ground my crotch into his lap, rubbing myself on his bulge and generally making a mess of his nice, pressed chinos. "Oh, I know you are."

"I am," he whimpered. John the Baptist buried his face between my breasts, kissing and licking them with endearing, puppylike enthusiasm.

Glancing back at Brian, I was pleased to see he'd taken up where I'd left off and had his dick in his hand, stroking. "He's just as bad as the rest of us." I grinned and rolled my hips.

The truth was, this whole thing was turning me on a lot more than I cared to admit. It was all very well pretending to be the whore of Babylon, but it didn't help when John the Baptist burrowed under my dress and slid his clever little fingers into my cunt.

"God, Candice! You aren't wearing any—"

"I believe that is what's commonly known as the gates of hell, John. Are you sure you want to go there?"

"Oh, yeah."

Oh, yeah, indeed. He was very good with his fingers, but I didn't want to get too carried away with my back to poor old Brian. I climbed off the Baptist, and caught my breath.

"Gentlemen, I think this calls for some serious soul searching, and this just isn't the right place to do it. Follow me."

And they did, like lambs to the slaughter, straight into my all-black bedroom.

"I know what you both thought, the first time you came to

visit," I teased, shrugging off my dress. "And I can assure you, you were absolutely right."

Funnily enough, it was Brian who was tearing his clothes off while I was talking. "I knew what you were, Candice."

"Did you know, too?" I unbuttoned John's shirt. He shook his head like a little boy. It was impossible to resist; I kissed him and felt him shudder. "Mmm, I bet you always think the best of people, don't you?"

"John's only been with us a short time. He doesn't know what real sin is." It was Brian, coming up to me from behind. He was pressing his dick against my ass and kneading my tits.

My concentration was slipping. "Oh, I don't know..." I undid John's chinos and slid my hand down the front of his boxers (coordinated undies—who would have guessed!). "I'd say John is worldlier than you give him credit for."

"Is he hard, Candice?" The voice was a hiss, slithering past my ear as its owner rubbed his cock between my cheeks.

Now that was a new twist, I thought. Brian was full of surprises. "Why don't you find out for yourself?"

I took one of his hands off my tit and dragged it down to John's cock. He wrapped his hand around it immediately.

John's eyes flew open and he gasped. "No, Brian...no." He wrapped his arms around my neck.

"Shh, Mister Baptist." I kissed him again and licked his lips. "There's really no point in doing things by half, is there?"

I got a series of little moans in response. John was thrusting his cock upward, into Brian's fist. The precum was smearing my stomach. It was messy, but hot, very hot. I cupped my hands over John's nice, taut ass, and felt his muscles flex as he bucked.

It was Brian who pushed us onto the bed—John underneath me and Brian on top. These boys were very close to the edge. I could tell by the way they were panting and moving. It pained me to think it was all going to end in a harmless little scrimmage; that would have been way too easy to dismiss as accidental. I wanted them steeped in viscous, gooey transgression.

"There isn't nearly enough real sin going on here," I protested. "Brian, get off me for a sec."

He slid off to one side, obediently. I rummaged for lube in the mess on my bedside table.

I looked down at John the Baptist and grinned. "I feel like sinning real bad, don't you?"

"Yeah, real bad."

"Mmm, good," I purred and eased my slick cunt onto him. Oh, you have no idea how good a real, honest-to-goodness Bible-thumping Christian feels sliding in. My pussy wrapped around his dick, swallowing it, clutching it. "Now you're really going to burn in hell, John."

"I know," he moaned and started to move.

I turned my head and pushed the tube of lube at Brian. "Know what to do with that?"

He smiled and nodded. Why wasn't I surprised?

The head of his cock was cool and slick as he got behind me and teased my hole with his cockhead. He pushed slowly, and I gasped as the tip popped inside my ass. He pumped farther into me with each stroke, opposing every thrust from John. I could hear Brian over my shoulder, whispering every dirty word ever invented. It was truly delicious, being sandwiched between the faithful. In fact, it was altogether too good.

Then, I was screaming, coming in a blind fury of pleasure, and I felt John shudder, jerk, and flood me. A moment later, Brian roared and thrust deep, twitching as he filled my ass.

We lay in a panting heap for a while. I think we were all just reveling in so much yummy sin. Finally, we fell apart.

"So, am I saved?"

"I don't think so, Candice," said John, nuzzling my nipple. "With certain people, it can take a long time."

Brian stretched and rolled onto his side. "Souls as black as yours, Candice, can take years."

It was odd. After that, they never really left; they just kind of moved in. The Witnesses did send a few more people around to see what had befallen their brethren, but there was a hushed conversation at the front door and we never heard from them again.

That's what convinced me I was right. Somewhere, there is a central registry of sinners.

ERICA'S JOHN

Erica K.

Tonight, my little slut, you're going to learn to suck cock."

Mistress Amanda sipped her red wine, smiling at me over the rim as she saw my eyes go wide. I could feel my own cock stir inside the tight panties I wore, the sensitive head rubbing against the lace. I could feel my nipples harden under the soft inserts that tented the spandex minidress I wore. My face flushed hot and I felt my head spinning. I struggled to find words.

"But Mistress," I began nervously.

"Silence!" snapped Mistress Amanda. "You said you wanted to learn to be a slut, and all sluts suck cock. You want to be a slut, don't you? That means learning to suck cock."

I felt my heart pounding. I had been coming to see Mistress Amanda for three months, with the guarantee, in our initial meeting, that she would teach me not only how to be a woman, but how to be a slut. I had never sucked cock before. I didn't consider myself bisexual. But my agreement with Mistress Amanda was that she owned me totally during these sessions. I trusted her ability to turn me into the slut I longed to be, but it would only work if I cooperated.

"Yes, Mistress," I said. "I want to learn to suck cock."

I had admitted it, weeks ago. Having dressed me up in panties and a bra and helped me shave my body smooth, Mistress Amanda had lashed me to her St. Andrew's cross and teased me with the pinwheel while asking me questions about what it meant to be a slut. I told her sluts got fucked, sucked cock, ate pussy. They did it with anyone. They loved every minute of it.

She'd grabbed my hair and forced my head back, her breath warm on my neck as she'd growled into my ear.

"That means you're going to suck cock, Erica. You're going to suck a man's hard cock."

"Yes, Mistress," I'd said. At the time, my cock had grown so hard in my panties that it hurt as it rubbed against the wooden cross, and the lace abraded it as I squirmed. I pictured myself down on my knees, my slut-painted lips closed around the shaft of a firm, erect cock. It sent a shiver through me, even as it scared me.

"Today's the day you learn how to give head, Erica."

"Y-yes, Mistress," I said nervously.

Mistress Amanda curled up on the couch next to me, cupping my cock and balls as she grinned wickedly. "I've got a man in the next room waiting for you," she told me. "He's got a nice, big, long, fat cock. Eight inches, Erica. Do you think you can handle it?"

"I—I don't know," I said.

"Oh, you'll handle it," she grinned. "You'll take that cock all the way down your throat, Erica. And that's when you'll be a slut. He's a very considerate man," she continued. "He'll be gentle. That is, until he's got you broken in. Then, he'll be very rough. That's what you want, isn't it, Erica?"

I'd said that, too. As she'd run the pinwheel over my balls, piercing the ephemeral lace of the panties I wore, Mistress Amanda had asked me whether men were rough or gentle with sluts.

"Very rough," I'd moaned. "They treat them like whores."

"How hard do they fuck sluts?" Mistress Amanda had cooed into my ear.

"Very hard," I'd breathed. "They fuck them so hard it hurts. They fuck them so hard they cry."

"But do they like it? The sluts? Do sluts like to get fucked so hard it hurts? Does a slut really *love* to get fucked so hard she cries?"

Now the time had come and I could hardly breathe; my head was spinning. I was more than a little nervous about doing this wicked thing, about going deeper into my role as Erica than I'd ever gone before. But it excited me. My nipples felt so hard I could almost believe they really capped the little A-cup inserts Mistress Amanda had me wearing. I looked at her with love and surrender.

"Yes, Mistress," I said.

This was the sluttiest outfit Mistress Amanda had ever had me wear. The spandex minidress was so tight it showed the sculpted nipples of my insert right through the material, even through the bra that held them. It was so short that the lace tops of my black seamed stockings showed right where the garters hooked onto them. It was so short, in fact, that my cock, bound back into the panties and throbbing hard, threatened to show underneath the hem.

"Come with me," Mistress Amanda said, taking my hand and leading me down the hall to her second bedroom.

I felt a flush of pride as I walked delicately on the four-inch heels of my fuck-me pumps. That had been one of the conditions of Mistress Amanda's training. "Sluts wear fuck-me pumps," she'd told me. "Sluts learn to walk in high heels."

Except this slut was six-and-a-half-feet tall when she wore four-inch fuck-me heels, so she towered over her mistress, who was only five-four in her stilettos. But there was no question that, spiritually, Mistress Amanda towered over me.

As Mistress Amanda led me down the dimly lit hallway, I felt a rush of lust for her. She wore a skintight black dress herself, this one ankle-length but slit all the way up to her hip. It even showed the side of the black thong she wore underneath. The dress was so tight that it clung to the firm swell of her ass, the cheeks well defined under the skintight satin. I could see the cleft between them, and I wanted it. I had spent many long hours between those cheeks, my tongue working Mistress Amanda's asshole, learning how to pay homage to her with my tongue in her dirtiest, most forbidden spot. I had also spent many hours between her legs, learning how to bring her to orgasm with my tongue.

Mistress Amanda had also spent hours cradling my face between her breasts, instructing me in the finer points of how a slut sucks another girl's tits. Mistress Amanda's C-cup breasts were exquisitely sensitive, and her hard nipples reacted so strongly to my carefully instructed ministrations that she could come just from that. I'd made Mistress Amanda come many times by sucking her tits. Just thinking about it made me want to soil my panties with my masculine come.

But the most pleasure I'd ever felt was when she'd stripped naked, strapped on her cock, and guided me onto the thick silicone member, teaching me how to suck. That had taken many, many hours, and now I knew I'd learned well.

"Here you go," said Mistress Amanda. "I'll be watching on the monitor. If I see you slacking off or not properly sucking cock..."

My rear cheeks gave a little clench as I remembered the many times Mistress Amanda had paddled my ass as she'd taught me how to properly eat her pussy. I learned quickly, but not quickly enough to avoid a few spankings.

"I'll suck good cock, Mistress," I said. "I promise."

"You'd better," said Mistress Amanda sternly. "And you won't forget to deep-throat him, will you?

I breathed heavily. "No, Mistress," I said. "I won't forget to deep-throat him."

"Good. Now go inside and introduce yourself to John."

"Yes, Mistress."

I reached out for the doorknob.

I gasped as I felt the Mistress's firm swat on my spandex-clad ass.

"Uh-uh," she snapped. "Where do sluts belong?"

I swallowed.

"On their knees," I sighed.

"That's right, Erica. *Crawl.*"

My cock surging in my panties, I obediently lowered myself onto my knees.

Then, I opened the door and began to crawl into the room on all fours.

The room where John was waiting to fuck my face.

Mistress Amanda closed the door behind me, and I heard a click as she locked it from the outside.

On my hands and knees, I could feel John's imposing male presence, and it both frightened and aroused me. I could smell the male sweat mingling with the scent of decidedly masculine cologne. I had never sucked cock before—not *real* cock. Now, I was about to become a real slut.

I looked up discreetly and saw the dark form of John sitting in the big armchair Mistress Amanda had so often occupied as she taught me to eat her pussy. The room was dimly lit, so I couldn't see him well, but he had a dark beard and a huge bulge in what looked like a filthy pair of blue jeans, which were tucked into black leather knee-high biker boots. I felt a surge of nervousness as I realized that John already had a hard-on.

I crawled over to John and curled up between his spread knees, putting my face in his lap.

"Hello," I said, remembering the Mistress's instructions that I introduce myself. "I'm Erica."

"You're my cocksucking slut," he growled. "Is that right?"

I felt a twinge of nervousness: something was familiar about the voice. I didn't dare look up at John's face. I just swallowed hard and nodded. "Yes," I said.

"You better do it real good," said John. "I paid Amanda twenty bucks to get your pretty little virgin mouth, slut."

A warmth went through my body as I heard those words. I was a virgin. I was about to suck cock for the first time. I breathed John's scent and again felt the nagging sense of something familiar hovering under the cheap cologne. My eyes flickered up and a bolt of shock exploded into me.

My cock immediately stiffened until it pulsed in agony, imprisoned in my panties. I smiled up at John, my full, red-painted lips feeling ready and hungry for him.

"I'll do it good," I promised. "I'll suck you real good, John."

"Then get to it, slut. I haven't got all day."

I buried my face in John's crotch, smelling the intense scent of filthy male sweat. I pressed my lips against the hard bulge in his jeans, leaving lipstick kisses up and down the length. I reached up and began to undo his belt.

"Just what I like," he said. "A girl who knows how to get down to business."

I took John's zipper down and pressed my face against his

filthy white underwear. The scent of male crotch was so overwhelming that it sent a fresh surge of excitement through me. I began to kiss and suck his cock through his jockey shorts, breathing deeply so I could smell him. Then I kissed my way up his waistband, where the tip of his fleshy knob showed over the white cotton.

"Suck it," he told me.

I pulled down his underwear and began to kiss the head. I could taste the sharpness of unwashed cock, the pungency of male essence. I could even taste a little come dried on the head, as if he'd just spurted recently and rubbed it all over him. I took his cock into my mouth and began working it.

John moaned, running his hands through my hair, careful not to dislodge the blonde bobbed wig that I wore. But he had a firm enough hold on my hair that I knew he wasn't going to let me up until I'd finished the job. My lips worked up and down his shaft, leaving streaks of lipstick along it. I felt my heart pounding, my arousal soaring as I gave myself over to the taste of his cock. I reached up to play with his nipples as I sucked him, and he slapped my hands away.

"No touching," he said. "Sluts don't touch. They just suck."

I put my hands, inert, between my slightly spread knees as I used my mouth on John. I felt his head pressing against the back of my throat, and I knew it was time to deep-throat him, as Mistress Amanda had instructed me to do. I took a deep breath and opened my mouth wide around his cock, forcing myself down onto it. Mistress Amanda had instructed me many times in the proper way to deep-throat a dildo, but John's cock was thicker and fuller than hers. I struggled to get it down my throat, feeling my gag reflex tightening my muscles as I refused to give up.

Finally, my throat slid down over John's cock. He sighed.

"You deep-throat pretty good," he said. "You must really want to be a slut."

I couldn't nod, couldn't say a thing. All I could do was work my mouth and throat up and down on John's cock.

When I came up for air I panted, my lungs burning. My throat felt wide and open. As I sank back down on John's cock, he took hold of my head and began to push his hips forward.

"Time for a throat-fucking," he growled.

He held me tight as his hips worked back and forth, shoving his cock into my throat. I struggled to open wide and take his powerful thrusts. After the first few, it proved easy, and I felt my arousal mounting as John used my face and throat.

When he pulled me off of him, I could feel long dribbles of drool running down my chin and onto my cleavage. The slobber was pink with my destroyed lipstick, and I knew if I looked in the mirror I'd see my lips sprawled red and wet across my face. I smiled up at him.

"Amanda told me for another ten bucks I could have your virgin ass," he told me.

I couldn't suppress the moan of fear that came from my lips. Mistress Amanda had fucked my ass before, but John's cock was so much bigger than hers.

"I figure that ass of yours is worth at least ten bucks. You gonna give it up to me, Erica?"

"Yes," I whimpered.

"Take off your panties and show me your ass."

My hands shaking, I reached under my tight dress and pulled off my panties, which Mistress Amanda always had me put on the outside of my garters. My cock sprang free, having slipped out of its lace prison—but still held tight by the cock ring and ball stretcher that I always wore when I was Erica. I turned around, putting my upper body on the floor and reaching behind me to lift my dress. I parted the cheeks of my shaved ass and showed my pink, virgin asshole to John.

"Nice," he said. "I'm going to enjoy this, Erica."

I felt the cold drizzle of lube between my cheeks, smelled the latex of a condom, then felt John's cockhead opening up my anus. I held my breath for a moment as his head pressed firmly against my opening, and then, as Mistress Amanda had instructed, I pushed myself back onto him, exhaling.

I gasped as I thrust myself onto John's thick organ. The sensations were so intense that I felt tears forming in my eyes, ruining my mascara. But I didn't stop. I pushed myself onto his cock until I felt my cheeks pressing against the rough fabric of John's filthy jeans.

"Nice," he said. "A slut who really wants it up the ass."

John came off the chair and pushed me down against the ground. He grabbed my head and forced it into the floor as his cock began to savage me, sliding smoothly in and out of my ass. He moaned loudly, reaching down to grasp my tightly bound cock and balls. The pressure of his hand was enough to make me realize I was going to come—despite the painful bondage imposed on my genitals.

"I'm gonna shoot in your fucking ass, slut. You want to come with me, Erica?"

"Yes," I moaned, choking back a sob as John began to viciously pump my cock with his hand. The painful stretch of my balls always made it hurt when I came, but my orgasm was always intensified tenfold. I anticipated my explosion with fear and excitement, and as John plumbed my ass I heard him groaning in orgasm, shooting deep inside me just as I came. The agony and pleasure mingled as they pulsed deep inside my body, and I felt hot streams of jizz soaking the front of my dress. John kept fucking me until he'd emptied himself, and then he sighed as he pulled himself out of me.

He sat back in the armchair and snapped his fingers.

"Come over here, Erica," he told me. "Put your head in my lap."

I obeyed, finding it hard to move after the intense ass-fucking I'd just received. But I wanted very much to tell John I loved him.

I pressed my head into John's lap and looked up, the recognition now overwhelming. I could smell my wife's pussy, ripe and raw, overpowering even the strong scents of cologne, of male sweat, of my own ass fucked wide open and glistening on the strap-on dildo.

"I love you, Erica. You know that, don't you?"

I smiled up into Jen's bright eyes, admiring the perfect line of the spirit-gummed beard, the familiar scent of my own crotch on the filthy jeans. I might have wondered why Mistress Amanda had instructed me to wear the same pair of jeans and the same pair of jockey shorts for a full month whenever I wasn't at work—why she'd instructed me to work out in them, jerk off in them, soak the underwear and jeans with my come and then hang them out to dry.

I might have even wondered why for our last session, the night before, she'd instructed me not to wash for several days beforehand and then rubbed the dildo all over my crotch and made me jerk off onto it, smearing the come into it.

And, more importantly, I might have wondered why Jen had been so mysterious lately, disappearing twice a week for a "class" she wouldn't tell me about. I might have wondered if she'd been having an affair, if the burden of having a husband who preferred to be Erica rather than Eric had proved too much for her and she'd sought the comforts only a "real" man could offer. I might have wondered that, but I didn't. Because I'd long since learned to trust the women in my life, however dangerous that trust sometimes felt.

When I'd confessed to Jen a year ago that I longed to become a slut, that I fantasized and dreamed of becoming "Erica" part of the time, she couldn't have been more supportive. There wasn't a hint of disappointment or anger in her tender eyes as she kissed me and told me that she loved me whoever I was.

Jen isn't a perfumed and primping straight girl, you see. Bicycling shorts are more her style than lace panties, and I don't think she's ever worn panty hose. High heels? Forget it. In the six years we've been together, I've seen her wear makeup once: at her sister's wedding. She had to have her best friend put it on for her, and even then it looked bizarre on her aquiline features.

Don't get me wrong: she's all woman. Believe it or not, she's even all slut. But there was simply no way that my wife was going to be able to teach me how to be the kind of slut I wanted to be, because her kind of slut sucked cock without lipstick, and when she went without panties it was under baggy jeans or cotton cargo pants.

And now I understood part of the reason why, when she suggested that I start seeing a professional, her one condition was that I tell her every detail of our sessions after I came home. Why she perked up noticeably when I mentioned that Mistress Amanda had told me I would suck cock. It wasn't just the pyrotechnic sex we would have whenever I described my submission to Mistress Amanda. No, I know now that there was much more going on.

And I know why I trusted her when she disappeared to her "class." Because she wasn't having an affair—yet. But she was planning one.

With Erica.

I looked up into my wife's eyes and smiled.

"How about we go home, Eric?"

"I'd like that very much, Jen."

"One condition," she said. "You promise to put the dress back on after we get home, little slut."

I buried my face in Jen's crotch and kissed her thighs. "Yes, Master," I told her. "I'll put the dress back on. I'll be your slut whenever you want."

Mistress Amanda was smiling ear to ear as we walked out.

FIRST TIME

Amy Wadhams

A blast of music assaulted us as Michelle and I entered the club. The pulsating beat of the techno combined with the flashing, spinning, multicolored lights, pounded through my system, intoxicating me. We nodded to the owner, a friend, and took up our usual seats. We took in all the new faces and old dotting the crowd in Club Rainbow.

We ordered our drinks, and jumped on the rather empty dance floor. For some reason, the lesbians at this place were always reluctant to dance, so we took it upon ourselves to give them something to watch. Gyrating, writhing, rubbing against each other, we filled the dance floor with our pent-up hormones. We were horny eighteen-year-olds looking to dance away our frustrations. We kissed, pushed each other up against the mirrored wall that lined the dance floor, and mimed every sex act we could think of.

When we had sufficiently petted each other, we returned to our table to catch our breath and down a Corona apiece, and then work on the Jell-O shots that the owner had kindly sent our way. As my last Jell-O shot slid pleasingly down my throat, I heard Michelle gasp lightly. I turned my head, following her gaze, to see a figure leaning against the wall, near the entrance.

I exhaled an appreciative breath and devoured this person with my eyes. Short, buzzed-off blonde hair; baggy, black clothing, and the face of a Botticelli angel. Michelle leaned over and said, "Is that a boy or a girl?"

"I think it's a boy," I said, feeling a warm tingle begin to spread throughout my pelvic region. I hoped it was a boy.

"Whatever it is," continued Michelle, "they're hot." I nodded my agreement, and returned to my libations, deciding that tequila was next in line for the night. After we had matched each other a few shots, we returned to the dance floor, which had acquired a few inhabitants after we had broken it in. We mixed ourselves into the mass of tangled bodies and began to dance anew, enmeshed, limbs and mouths reaching out and stroking body parts unseen.

I had my head thrown back, arms gently raised, and was bouncing my hips in time to the beat of a slower song, simply allowing the alcohol and vibrations to guide me, lost in the sensations around me, when a hand encircled my waist from behind. I was pulled slowly back, never breaking my rhythm, and the back side of my body came into contact with the front of someone else's. Someone who had soft breasts that flattened gently against my back. The person's groin pressed against my ass, following my movements, and I felt something there.

It felt like a dick, but too hard, too perfect. I lowered my hands, and reached back to slide them down the person's lithe, sinuous body. When I reached the person's hips, I felt the harness of a strap-on. I turned my head, glancing over my shoulder, and saw that my mysterious dance partner was the person whose gender we had just been debating. She leaned her head forward and nuzzled my neck, as her hips followed mine, her dick sliding over my asscheeks as if seeking entrance.

We danced and danced, her hands gripping my hips, then sliding up and over my breasts, then down my arms to interlace her fingers with mine. She kept her body molded to mine, her mouth at first brushing against the nape of my neck, then sliding around between my jaw and my shoulder and feathering kisses that had me biting my lip in ecstasy.

After an endless time of pure awareness of each other, I turned, and our bodies met again. I met her blue eyes, topped by a small silver eyebrow ring. I bit my lip as I drank in her perfect lips and sinner's eyes, then stood on tiptoe to reach her ear and whispered, "My name is Amy."

She turned her head slightly, so that her hot breath met my ear, and replied, "I'm Tracy." She placed a light kiss under my ear, and then skimmed her lips over my jaw to hover over my mouth for a moment. We both stood there, locked together on the dance floor, lips millimeters apart, breath coming hard and fast. Then she closed the gap. Our lips met and an explosion went off inside of me. I'd kissed plenty of girls in my time, and enjoyed the hell out of it every time. But never before like this. Her tongue begged entrance, and I parted my lips. We dueled, fought, parried, and thrusted, growing more heated with every moment.

Finally we drew apart, shy smiles spreading across our faces. I looked around and noticed Michelle sitting at our table, laughing and giving me a thumbs-up. I blushed and took Tracy's hand. We walked over to the table, and I introduced Michelle to Tracy. We spent the next few hours laughing, drinking, and dancing. Tracy was raw with sexuality, and had a quick, dry humor. We enjoyed her company, and when it came time to go, I unreservedly asked to see her again. We set up a time to meet at the club the next week. Tracy walked me out to Michelle's car, and pinned me to it, her strap-on grinding into me delightfully as we kissed ravenously.

The whole following week, I could think of nothing but Tracy. My mind switched from panicked doubts of my sexuality to vivid fantasies of us fucking in every way I could think of. When the day finally arrived, I prepared myself fully, shaving my pussy, wearing my best lingerie, and choosing just the right clothes. For the whole drive to Houston, Michelle and I laughed and acted like idiots, as usual, but inside I was quivering with anticipation.

When we arrived at the club, we found Tracy upstairs waiting. We passed the night much as we had the week before, slamming back as much liquor as we could hold down, chatting with each other, and hammering our bodies together in the twisted sea of humans on the dance floor. Only this time when it was closing time, Tracy took my hand and led me to her car instead of Michelle's. I got in, and as we drove to her apartment, her hand played up and down my thigh.

Once we reached her place, she bashfully showed me around, ending in the bedroom. Licking my lip, and drawing on all my courage, I sat on her bed and slowly looked up at her through a veil of lashes. She stood watching me as I hooked a finger through her belt loop and pulled her to me. Her lips parted as I unbuckled her belt, and unfastened her jeans. I had to see what she was packing.

I was not disappointed. When I drew down her pants and boxers, a thick pink strap-on leapt out to meet me. In a haze of lusty curiosity, I reached out and ran my hands over it. Tracy's breath hitched, and she pushed me back on the bed and slithered onto it next to me. Hastily, our clothes were torn off and abandoned.

When we were completely undressed, she propped herself up over me, and our mouths met as our hands explored the planes of each other's bodies. We grasped at breasts, nipples becoming handles to be turned and pulled. Her hand traveled down to stroke the silky smooth skin of my mound. Her deft fingers then dipped in, testing, finding a molten wetness aching for her expert touch.

Then she maneuvered her way down, until her face was hovering above my pussy. My head flew back, and a cry escaped me as she parted my lips with her tongue. An indescribably miraculous sensation flooded my body as I felt her tongue begin to glide across my clit and opening. The light, velvety pressure of her tongue left a trail of singing nerve endings in its wake. When her tongue entered me, I gripped the sheets, calling out her name.

She continued to taste and tease, building an inferno inside of me. When I was panting and shaking, near orgasm, she leaned back and gave me a feral grin, glossy with my juice. She licked her lips and came back up beside me.

She knelt beside my head and positioned her dick beside my face. "Get it wet," she said in a soft yet steely voice. I opened my mouth and took it in, coating it with saliva, licking at it. After a moment, she pulled out, and lay atop me. I spread my legs, and she dipped her head for a scorching kiss as she slowly penetrated me. I cried out, lost in the feeling of soft lips, supple mounds of breast pressed to mine, and hardness pounding into me.

She reached down with one hand and rubbed my clit as she thrust, sending me over the edge of orgasm faster than I had ever gone before. When the last shudder had left me, she rolled to the side. I caught my breath and sat up. I pulled the strap-on off of her and nestled myself between her legs. I was finally going to do something I had been dreaming of.

I bent forward, and she inhaled sharply as I laid a kiss just under her belly button. I slid down farther and lightly stroked my lips and jaw across her lower lips. I drank in the warm wet scent of her, then spread her open and placed my tongue against her clit. I began tracing around it and her opening, noting the places that merited extra moans of pleasure from her. I began flicking my tongue across her clit, increasing the pleasure, as I ran my hand up her thigh.

I lowered my tongue and dipped in and out of her, swirling to reach every point I could. When she was as wet as she could be, I returned my tongue to her pleasure button and slid a finger into her, reaching, thrusting, bending to hit that one magical spot inside her. Her back arched as I sped my tempo, having found just the right places to tease.

I felt the spasms and tightening in her sheath as orgasm spilled across her, and I pressed her G-spot harder and faster and sucked her clit into my mouth. She groaned through gritted teeth as her body trembled in release. I kept going until she fell limp. I pulled back, my face slick with rain-scented juices, and withdrew my glistening fingers. She reached for one of our discarded pieces of clothing, and we wiped off the excess fluids, then I lay next to her.

She drew me into her arms, my back to her front. I knew as I drifted off that everything had changed. I wasn't the same person that I had been at the beginning of that night. I knew in the morning I would feel the return of the doubts, the questioning of myself. But at that moment, I was perfectly happy.

GONE HUNTIN'

Anusha Ramkissoon-Forte

I'D RATHER BE HUNTIN'. That's what the bumper sticker on your truck says. Do you mean it? Really mean it?

You're reluctant as hell to talk to me. I wonder if I freak you out that much. I guess I'm nothing like your kind of woman, am I? Too much eyeliner? Or is it the striped leg warmers, the red leather jacket?

Don't worry about it, *babe*; when the clothes come off it's all the same underneath. Except maybe for the nipple rings...and all the tattoos. They aren't that scary when you touch them, though.

And I think you want to touch.

I know that look in your eyes; I know that smile you try to play off. Your kind isn't that hard to read—and we're all the same really. Girls and boys, just different bits. The same instinct drives us all. Makes us want.

You feel sexy when I look at you, when my gaze trails down your arms—big ol' arms stretching your T-shirt sleeves tight, curly golden hair bright against your tan.

Don't look so self-conscious as you sip your beer. Sure, I said this shit tastes like horse piss. It does. When you've had a chance to lick a good burgundy or a rosé off my naked skin you'll understand. Maybe we'll even compromise: Jim Beam Black Label.

Now, at the mention ol' JB, I can see the possibilities. I wish I could show you them tonight, but it's too soon, way too early for that. I've barely got you baited, taking hesitant steps in my direction while I wait. I'm lettin' you come to me.

Of course I'll do a shot with you. Are you testing me out now? I can hold my own against the bleach-blonde biker babes with the husky voices and the bustiers, the kind that you hunt. You like them because they're tough; you look at me and think I'm soft. But have any of them ever sipped absinthe all night long and watched the moon until it faded into the rising sun of a cold dawn?

I want to do that with you.

Oh, man, I'm getting way, way ahead of myself here.

Maybe I should just take it slow. Do the shot and subside into my chair in the shadows. Let you talk football with my brother while I look out at the wind stirring up the lake and the raccoons digging through the bushes at the side of the restaurant. God, the little buggers are fat. They must live on leftover wings and fried pickles. So not good for them at all…

Your voice pulls me away from raccoons and night, reminding me of how damp my panties are under this Lolita skirt. Staring at your mouth, your curvy soft lips so at odds with that Paul Bunyan jaw and those great big shoulders, doesn't help either my panties or concentration, and I ogle like a fool.

Would I like what?

"She's not listening," Jimmy says, and he rolls his eyes.

I turn my gaze back to yours. "Yeah. I'm sorry, I wasn't. What's going on?"

Jimmy answers. "Dale was saying we could start work on that deck of yours next week."

The deck Jimmy promised, to which you simply said, "Okay," and shrugged your shoulders, not really caring either way. And now you've brought it up again. Now. Long after the rest of us have forgotten.

I don't take my eyes from you, and you don't say anything more. You watch me, silent, sizing me up.

"Seriously?" I ask. "Do you guys have the time?"

Jimmy nods. "Should just take us a couple weekends." He keeps on going, keeps on talking: posts and cement and wood treatments and bricks. Stuff that means jack shit to me really, but you smile as he rambles.

Do you know that I'm thinking this means I'll finally have you on my turf, on my time? Did you think that too? Is that why you reminded him about building the silly thing? Your blue eyes are so hard to read, hiding behind that glass and that scruffy baseball cap. How much else are you hiding behind your carpenter jeans and your rough façade?

Are you going to let me find out?

The weather's starting to cool down; it's almost hunting season. I stand out on the deck in the blue light of evening, shiny new boards under my bare feet, thinking there are little pieces of you tangled in this deck. You wouldn't think of it like that, in terms of sweat and blood and DNA, but you know it just the same.

Weekend after weekend now I've watched you, sun beating on your naked back. Watched your hands, the way they move, the way you scratch your head and swing your tools. I've looked and I've listened; I've followed and I've tracked. And now I'm ready to bring you down. If only you'll just let me.

"Looks good," you say and I wonder: are you talking about me or the deck? It's just us here. So very kind of you to let Jimmy leave and stay behind to "finish up."

"Yep," I say. "I love it. Thank you so much, Dale."

You look at me and then glance away. "No problem," you say.

"Need help with all that?" I ask as you start to pick up your things. You smile and say, "Sure!" though we both know it's a lie.

You hand me a toolbox and power cord, teasing me now, asking me if I can handle all that without breaking. With the hand holding the power cord I flip you off, and you laugh. I follow you around the side of the house, wait while you load up the leftover decking, the tools, and your power saw. You dust your hands on your pants and take a deep breath.

The evening breeze is just a little bit cold, but I don't really need it. My nipples are getting hard all on their own. You notice, and I notice you noticing.

For a few smoking seconds we look at each other, thinking about possibilities, and then you mutter something about Jimmy. Oh, come on. Do you really feel guilty about screwing your buddy's little sister? Or are you just a teensy bit nervous about the pale, skinny chick who listens to death metal? Is that pushing your boundaries just a little too much?

I hope it is. Come on, babe, haven't you ever wanted to try something that scares you just a little bit? You're not the kind of guy to shy away from danger. If you were, I wouldn't have noticed you in the first place.

I say, "I owe you."

Surprised, you ask why.

"For the deck. What about I buy you a case of that horse piss you like so much?"

You lean on the tailgate and fold your arms.

"What about you buy me some of that fancy shit you like? I'm open to new experiences."

Oh, are you now? "Yeah? I might put that to the test."

The air seems to have gotten warmer all of a sudden. Or maybe it's just me.

Every breath has meaning, every little shift of your shoulders or my eyes. Here's where you get to show just how good those huntin' skills of yours are. One wrong move, one misinterpreted signal, that's all it takes to spook this moment, leave us both half-cocked and disappointed.

Can you bring me down? Are you gonna let me run?

You move and I tense. I can hear our breathing over the sound of crickets in the grass, over the sound of cars in the distance. The moment seems to hold, to stretch indefinitely out into the gathering dark. Muscles trembling with the strain, I wait.

But you don't make me wait too long.

The kiss is hard and urgent, like I thought it would be. As I wanted it to be. I dig my fingers into your neck, body arching, lips crushed against yours. Breathless. Desperate.

Wounded.

But you're not finished with me yet, are you?

I get my answer when I reach down and stroke my fingers along your crotch. I see you glance up and scan driveways, checking to see whether there's anybody outside observing this little transgression, but we're hidden well enough between the truck and the garage door. I rub a little harder, explore a little further, my fingers playing against denim stretched tight. You catch my wrist and hold my arm at my side, kissing me again.

I'm frustrated; I wasn't done yet.

"Easy there, girl," you tell me, laughing. "Inside first." Your voice isn't quite even, your breathing just a hair rougher than usual. I wonder if I've managed to put a fracture in your composure after all.

Destruction, that's me. Picking things apart to see how they work, putting them back together in my own image and likeness. A beautiful man once told me I had a god complex. He told me a whole lot more, explaining me, rationalizing me, trying to pin me down. The words rolled off his tongue and my skin like beads of sweat on a hot summer night. I forgot most of what he said.

Since you've got my arms pinned down, I push my tits against your chest.

"Damn, girl. You're a handful," you say.

Right in the middle of the living room you take off my shirt and pants, leaving dusty smudges on my skin and my favorite black silk panties. I take off your shirt and unbutton your fly. We aren't in this for romance; it's not needed. The hunt is brutal, frantic beauty.

Still, you lay me down on the floor and kiss my nipples, suck the metal penetrating the flesh as if you truly love the taste. When I moan and squeal, you smile. You turn me over and pull the soaked, dirty panties off.

"God, you got a fine ass."

I laugh and look at you over my shoulder, hair falling in my eyes, lips red without lipstick because I've been biting them so hard. Because you have that effect on me. Yeah.

Are you so surprised that I'm frozen and dazzled by you? That I'm caught?

On elbows and knees, the ass you like so much arched up in the air, I spread my knees. Flex my toes in anticipation. Your fingers explore my cunt: middle finger probing, index finger on my clit. Gripping my pussy like you own it, and I guess for now you do.

Who was hunting who anyway?

I don't know anymore. It feels so good, I've got to close my eyes while I clench tight around your touch, move my hips, rocking backward and forward on the sensation of work-roughened skin invading me, teasing me, cupping me, fucking me.

The phone rings. We ignore it. It rings again and again and again, but my moaning drowns it out. I look back again to see you take the baseball cap and throw it across the room, see you grab my ass with your other hand, holding me in place while you get me where you want me, not giving me a chance to breathe.

You pull your fingers out of me with a sweet plop, suck them off while you watch my expression, and I stare back, silly now with longing and lust. You seem to enjoy just kneeling there, just watching me and stroking your hard-on, you do it for so goddamn long.

Don't you know that thirty seconds of waiting for you to fuck me is an eternity? Don't you know how bad and for how long I've wanted you? Ever since you and Jimmy met, ever since I first saw you playing cards on his back porch shirtless and had to pretend I wasn't already weak-kneed with lust when I shook your hand.

Because, you know, I'm a lady after all.

Shaking your head, you pull my hips backward, guide your cock to my ready, waiting pussy, ease into me slowly, a little bit at a time. You're making me wait for it, making me want it. I think I'll die of frustration. And then before I know it, before I can make sense of it, we're fucking, rough, hurried thrusting, fucking with a purpose.

My tits sway painfully, but there's no time to slow down. The time for waiting, for baiting and measuring, is long, long gone, and I almost brain myself on the coffee table leg, but your hand is there to buffer the blow. You pull me back to you, take me down to the floor with you, spooning. You slide ever deeper in. I stretch one hand out, find the edge of the rug to pull and twist and abuse, while I move with you, counterpoint to you.

And you. Oh, you. Fucking me and kissing my neck and your hand moving across my chest, brushing my nipple rings. I'm ripping my fingernails into the rug like a cat. Coming and screaming and cum all down my legs. Sweaty, amazing, anything-but-gentle sex.

Just like I always knew it would be with you.

You lie on the rug, staring up at the ceiling miles above. You tell me: "I've gotta go."

I don't argue because the ceiling is spinning slowly in time with my head. I'm waiting for time to slow down so I can think again. But you mistake my silence and you try to explain. I know it's dark now, and there's no reason for your truck to still be in my driveway. The neighbors are nosy, and you don't want Jimmy to know after all.

I take a deep breath. It sounds like a sigh, but really I just need air. I turn my head to look at you and I roll my eyes.

"I don't think he cares."

"Oh, yeah, he does." Lying on your side, propped up on one elbow, jeans undone to show off your cock, still half-erect and smeared with me, you lean down and kiss my nose, just on the tip. I wrinkle it and you laugh.

"Besides," you say as you look me over, rumpled hair to toes curled with pleasure. Your voice is soft, thoughtful, but not disappointed. "I don't think I could…" Your words trail off; you laugh. "Nah. No way I could hold on to you. You'll be the one that gets away."

I slide closer and wriggle to fit my body beside yours. The hair on your chest tickles my cheek, and I can smell the scent of your body, sweat and sex and wood dust. I look up into your eyes. I'm not dazzled anymore, but I like the view. I've put you back together, almost the same, just a little edgier. A little sharper than before.

"Why are you complaining?" I say. "You'd rather be huntin', right?"

You don't say anything because you can't. I've got you fair and square and you know it. But you like it. And you just give me a guilty grin.

BALZAC'S MONSTER

Rebecca Boyd

He just left my house, and I want to write down what happened. I want to come so bad, harder than I've ever come before.

I play both sides—dominant and submissive—but recently I've had a regular partner who totally obsesses me. I do something with him I never would have thought I'd find hot, but I can't get it out of my mind; I get so turned on when I know he's coming over, sometimes it's a little bit scary.

His name is Mike and he's not what you would expect. Well, not that I'd know what you expect—but he's not what *I* expected. He's twenty-three and halfway between nerdy and gorgeous, with a good-looking face and blond hair and dweeby glasses. He's fairly athletic and muscular and I imagine if I were to get his clothes off and make love to him, his body would feel incredible up against mine. But I never will, which is why I'm so turned on by him.

He sees me about once a week. He comes over to my place,

which I always clear in anticipation of his arrival—it gives me a deadline, which helps me keep everything together.

I answer the door and he always looks me over with open lust. He doesn't need me to dress up for him; in fact, he kind of likes it if I don't. Most times I've seen him I've been wearing sweats and a tank top. Sometimes I don't even bother taking a shower. There's something so dirty and wicked about that, it makes it even hotter. Other times I don't wear much of anything, just a skimpy robe, so as soon as he's in the door I can let it fall open and he can see me and voice his excitement. I always laugh when he does.

Either way, it's obvious as soon as he's inside that he wants me, and wants me bad. After all, with the kind of relationship we have, there's no need for pretension. He comes in the door and I hug him and let him hold me a little, and I'm always sure to brush myself against him in just such a way that I feel his cock start to swell. When I feel him getting hard in his jeans, I flatten my palm against his cock and rub him harder. It's never long before he's fully erect. In fact, sometimes he's that way when I answer the door, which is gratifying in a different way. He always bends down to kiss me and I always pull back, smiling and sometimes laughing at him. That always makes his cock swell more.

Then, "You need a hand job," I tell him, or "Go get comfortable," or "I'm going to jerk you off now," or if I'm feeling dirty then, "I want to stroke that big cock of yours, baby," or if I feel especially evil and wicked, "Why don't you get naked, darling. I want to make love to you."

He always gets visibly turned on, blushes hot in the face, and goes to the living room. While he's undressing, I go to the kitchen and get him a beer. I also get a warm washcloth and put it in a closed bowl so it'll stay warm as long as possible. I take my time so that when I enter the living room, he's sitting naked in the easy chair, which I've draped with a soft cotton blanket. Next to the easy chair is a side table with a bottle of lube and a big box of tissues.

His cock strains hard against his belly. Sometimes he's stroking it.

If I discover him stroking it, I come up to him, laugh, lean over him, and slap his hand, hard. Sometimes I slap his cheek. Once I grabbed his throat, bent down low, and spat right in his face. Other times I just call him a pervert, or a fucking pervert or a disgusting jerk-off, and he shamefacedly takes his hand off his cock, which seems to throb with excitement at the abuse.

Then, smiling, I give him the beer.

Whatever I'm wearing, I take it off. He doesn't mind if I'm clothed, but I like to be naked, because it excites me that we're both nude, both ready to fuck—me more ready than him, truth be told—and we don't, because that's not what we do. *This*, instead, is what we do.

I take stock of his position, of the hardness of his cock and of his nipples, of what the look on his face tells me, and of what I want to do to him. Sometimes I tell him, "Spread your legs a little more," or "Lean forward a little." I sometimes say, "Show me your balls," and when he does, lifting them to display how hard and tight they are against the base of his cock, I laugh and say something like, "What do you know? They really are blue!" Then I laugh some more, while he goes red all over and breathes hard, and I go down on my knees.

He sips his beer and looks me over with open desire, hungry for my naked body. I wrap my hands around his cock. Usually I put one hand around the shaft and another open against the head, rubbing the glans. I stroke his cock up and down while I work the head with my palm. He's always so turned on that it doesn't take me long to coax moans out of him. He writhes while I stroke him until he's good and worked up, and then sometimes I take a break and caress his hard, muscled chest, playing with his nipples. A few times I've leaned forward and run my tongue from base to shaft, or even slid his cock into my mouth and caressed it a little with my tongue. It turns me on so much to feel it so hard against my lips and tongue. I never give him more than a few strokes with my mouth; I return to using my hands, and after my mouth comes off of him he always gasps, "Thank you!"

I always laugh, cruelly, wickedly. Then I grip his cock harder and start to stroke him toward orgasm.

He moans. I take a break and go back to caressing his chest and nipples. Sometimes I stand, climb into the chair, sit in his lap, and kiss him softly, feeling his naked body against mine and feeling his cock throbbing against my flesh. He moans and whispers, "Please!" He wants me. I always want to fuck him so bad it's making me crazy. But I'm not going to. I get back down and start caressing him again. At that point I usually add some lube, to prolong the hand job. I'm always very careful at that point, because if I make him come too fast I'll be robbing him of a valuable experience.

I slather him with lube, stroke his cock, touch his balls. When he's very close, I tease him with just the tip of my thumb until he's cooled down a little, and then I start all over again. Sometimes I make it last an hour; once, it was two.

When he's close, I laugh at him. I make him beg. "You want it, don't you, Mike?" I tell him. "You'd better ask for it."

"Please, Mistress," he moans. "Please make me come."

I *tsk*. "I don't think so," I say, or something like that. "I think you have it too easy. You come over to my house, drink my beer, and get a hand job...I think that's too easy, don't you?"

He shakes his head desperately. "No, Mistress, no. Please, please just let me come."

I smile at him, sometimes laugh. I add more lube and begin stroking his cock firmly up and down. Usually I do it with both hands, but sometimes I'm massaging his balls with my left, or flattening my palm against his perfect, muscular belly.

"Don't take your eyes off of me," I usually have to tell him, which I like. "Keep looking at me and I'll make you come."

I hold eye contact with him, and it makes me so wet to see his eyes all open and desperate and vulnerable. He's close—so close. I stroke him. I see his body shudder as he reaches the point of no return. He starts to feel it coming, the spasms deep inside him. He's going to finish. I'm going to finish him.

Then my hands come away, and I leave him there twisting. I watch him writhe and hear him cry out. At first he would break eye contact; now I've trained him not to look away. He just stares at me as he starts to come.

That's when my instincts take over: I need to see what he needs to totally ruin his orgasm.

Sometimes, I've timed it perfectly and I have to do nothing but look up into his eyes and smile and laugh as he convulses and his cock spurts all over his belly, with only the barest hint of pleasure flooding through him. I see the dismay breaking across his face and the frustration and anger growing as he realizes he's really not going to come—that his chance is gone. His orgasm is over, and he didn't feel it.

Other times, I've waited a fraction of a second too long, and if I don't do something he'll just come from his body's own momentum. I can tell it from the way he moves, the way he moans and breathes.

Those times, I have to do something to stop his pleasure. Sometimes I use my fingernails. I flick the most sensitive part of his cock, just behind the head on the underside, hard with my fingernails, and keep doing it so he cries out desperately in pain. Then he shoots but I can tell he feels no pleasure. Other times, I do it with my palm—a hard slap against his glans while I laugh.

Other times, I haven't gone far enough—he is about to come, right on the brink, but he hasn't made it. Then, I put my thumb against his glans and hold it, staring into his eyes and smiling evilly. I drape my fingers against his belly when I do it that way. He always spurts onto my fingertips. Those times, I make him lick them clean.

Once or twice, he's been so desperate to come that he reaches for his cock with his hand. Then, I grab his wrist and drag it away, and laugh as he twists against me. I always win, and he comes without coming; he spurts without feeling pleasure.

Oh, don't get me wrong. I'm not a monster. There's a *little* pleasure. But it's nothing like it would be if I stroked him through it. It's nothing like coming for real. His body releases his seed, but he doesn't get off.

And I can see the agony and shamed frustration on his face. He looks on the verge of tears. Twice, he's actually begun crying from the frustration. Would you think I'm horrible if I told you that turned me on?

Well, maybe I am a little bit of a monster.

I smilingly pull out some tissues and clean him up. Then I get the warm washcloth, which is usually not warm anymore if I've done my job right and teased him for a long time. I clean his softening cock all over, taking my time. If I do things correctly, sometimes he's good and hard by the time I'm finished.

When that happens, he usually starts to stroke himself desperately while he watches me get dressed. I watch with mounting arousal, knowing he'll never come.

"Put your clothes on," I tell him. "See you next week."

He gets up and dresses meekly. I sit in the easy chair, watching him with a cruel smile on my face. He looks back at me as he prepares to leave, as if to beg me for another hand job, or a chance to pleasure me. I'm so fucking close to coming that I would love to fuck him, or to let him get me off with his mouth or his hand or my vibrator.

But I don't. Instead, as he opens his mouth to beg and plead, I say coldly, "See you next week." He leaves obediently.

The door closes and the tension goes out of my body. I can never believe how fucking turned on I am. I'm going crazy by this point, invariably. I'm dripping wet and my clit is swollen and I'm so turned on I can feel the swell inside my abdomen that tells me my hormones are hungry for release. Whatever I'm wearing—robe, sweats, shorts, jeans, panties, little black dress—I wriggle out of it right there in the chair. I open the drawer of the side table and retrieve my favorite vibrator, a bullet with seven vibrating patterns. I always keep it there. I turn the vibrator on and slide the hard plastic bullet against my clit, sometimes using lube, sometimes using my fingers inside me, or pairing the vibrator with a dildo I keep in the side table, too. I start to fuck and tease myself to orgasm, which won't take long.

Mike's a writer, you see, now in his last few months of getting his MFA in fiction. He told me on our first "date" that he subscribes to Balzac's view that orgasms are creative energy, and to spend them recklessly means creativity is lost. I think he felt like he lost a little bit of his soul each time he came. "There goes another novel," Balzac once moaned after a visit to a brothel.

Balzac's *Human Comedy* was almost one hundred novels long—so if this is how he did it, he definitely created a monster.

But whatever the secret of writing one hundred novels, if Mike didn't spend somehow, he'd end up with the world's worst case of blue balls, and he'd be more distracted than energized. That wouldn't help him write. By teasing and tormenting him to orgasm, then ruining it, I spend the forces of his body but leave his soul hungry and wanting.

Like I said, I'm a switch. I never thought I would be this dominant, torturing a man I'm so attracted to, pleasuring him and then turning his pleasure to agony. But it works. Mike's broken through his longtime writer's block and written hundreds of pages on his novel since we started. I've read it. It's brilliant.

Meanwhile, doing this turns me on so much I can't stand it. Mike's usually not gone five minutes before I'm rising quickly toward my orgasm; sometimes I like to think I start so fast that he can hear the buzzing begin as he walks down the front stairs. Other times, I fantasize that he's paused outside, listening to me moan as I get ready to come.

That turns me on even more, that he's denied, but reaching for me. I always pulse toward orgasm, turning up the vibrator until I'm right on the brink. And then—

At the last moment, I pull away, switching off the vibe, spreading my legs to prevent the natural urge of my thighs to rub together. If I've timed it right, the spasms begin and the pleasure flares and then fades; sometimes I have to reach down and pinch my clit, or slap it, or pinch my nipples very hard so that even though my body releases, I don't feel the pleasure. Or, at least, I don't feel most of it.

I'm left gasping and panting and twisting and moaning, on the verge of tears from the frustration. I wanted to come, and I didn't. My body released, but I didn't feel the pleasure. Remember when I told you Mike cried twice and it turned me on? I've cried many more times than that. And it turns me on even more.

When I'm spent but not spent, I get up and take a nice long shower. I get dressed again, in shorts or sweats, something loose and easy and comfortable, because I've got a long haul ahead of me.

Then I go to my computer desk and start writing. Sometimes I can go for eight or ten hours after a session with Mike; it's agony, but I'm so filled with energy I can't resist the steady pulse of words, like the fuck I wanted but never got.

Mike's not the only one getting an MFA, see? Actually, that's how I know him. Would you think I'm a monster if I told you I'm his faculty adviser?

Maybe I *am* a little bit of a monster. And I think maybe Balzac was right.

HIGH-SPEED WIRELESS

Miranda Logan

They were still getting the hang of living together; the small apartment didn't help, and neither did their freakish schedules. During the days, Amy would work in cafes, assembling complicated flow charts and technical documents, while he slumbered away the exhaustion brought on by a four-to-midnight shift at the bakery or, battling said exhaustion with espresso and vigorous exercise, took Rocky down to the dog park to frolic with the other pooches owned by night-shifters. He respected her space and never called her on her cell phone, except that one time when Rocky cut his foot and needed to be rushed down to the pet hospital.

Instant messaging, however, was an entirely different matter. Amy tolerated his occasional IMs about what he should make for dinner, whether she minded if he painted the bathroom blue, or whether it was Curt Jurgens or Harvey Kruger in *The Enemy Below*. Only occasionally did she curse the proliferation of high-speed wireless Internet.

And as a matter of fact, on days like this, when she was wasting time waiting for the inspiration to hit—the kind of inspiration that technical writers can sometimes (particularly on Wednesdays) only long for, the deep and passionate hunger to complete a challenging and utterly unappealing task—she often found herself sitting there waiting for him, wishing he'd pop up with *is it kale or chard u hate? I cant remember.*

This particular Wednesday in the Breault's Cafe on Bourbon Street, when the familiar chime sounded in her headphones mingled with the languid rhythms of Loup Garou, he wasn't asking about kale or chard.

Instead, *u r wearing your cherries* was what she got, at the critical moment where she was trying to decide whether she should read the headlines on Google News for the fourth time or email her friend in Australia about the last Harry Potter novel.

It took her a minute to realize what the fuck he meant. She was, to her knowledge, not wearing actual cherries, nor had she ever worn them, except that one time in Napa when the B&B had provided a seasonal fruit basket. Then she recalled with a sudden rush of annoyance that she was, in fact, wearing her cherries.

He was referring to her white cotton thong with the silk-screened pair of cherries, a teasing gift from Mike in the early days of their relationship. Quite a few not-very-amusing jokes had passed between them about that particular pair of underwear ("yeah, right!" "adaptive camouflage," "false advertising," and, the most raunchy, "I see there are two of them," snicker snicker). She wasn't sure if it was the fact that he'd bought them for her or the fact that, more than occasionally, he liked her to play the virgin—okay, *she* liked to play the virgin—that made them such a frequent topic of conversation. They were the only piece of sexy lingerie Mike had ever given her, but she ascribed that more to his low-paying job than to any lack of interest in her sweet nothings. Still, they had a certain sentimental value, which had led them to be the only clean pair of underwear in her top drawer when she'd gotten dressed to come to the cafe this morning.

Yeah, she messaged him back, a trifle perturbed that he'd played fetch for three hours with Rocky yesterday instead of doing laundry. *So?*

There was a long pause, and Amy sat there waiting. Toward the end of the wait, she regretted the snarky tone of her message, hungry for human contact to shroud her from the flow charts that threatened to consume her.

Sassy, Mike IMed her back, perturbing her still more. *U R wearing ur low cut jeans. Some1 might see.*

Christ, it annoyed her when he used that Internet lingo crap. Her boss in North Carolina pulled the same shit on her, everything *oic* and *lmkhig* and *wtf,* making her have to read every message three times before she had any idea what the fuck either of them was talking about. *SPEAK ENGLISH,* she typed in bold capital letters, then erased it and thought for a minute.

She glanced over her shoulder, noticing that the low-cut jeans she wore—another holdover from the clean-clothes pile, something she rarely wore because they showed off way too much of her ass—had ridden down as she'd wriggled, bored, in her seat. The white string of the cherried thong stuck high above the waistband, and probably had for quite some time. She'd gotten fairly used to butt floss, but this was something else entirely.

Amy was not really an exhibitionist. She did not flash at Mardi Gras, did not dance on tables like Paris Hilton, did not wear her one pair of low-riders except on laundry day. She had only once sunbathed in the nude, and still worried that the perverts up on the cliff overlooking the nude beach had posted photos of her on the Internet and some day she was going to get a phone call from Mom informing her that Dad had dropped dead from a heart attack while cruising for porn on the Internet. Amy didn't mind people looking, but any illicit thrill that such a thing provided was compromised by her need for personal space.

Mike, on the other hand, was quite the voyeur, and there was something about the turn-on he got from seeing her exposed that tempted and enticed her. She indulged it occasionally, but his frequent suggestions that he finger her in the movie theater or go down on her on the streetcar were met with icy silence.

Still, she was bored as hell, and after all, she didn't really need to get this flow chart to her boss until tomorrow. Besides, it *was* Mardi Gras season, and she was sort of considering letting Mike's persuasion work its magic on her at the parade.

So, after erasing her bitchy response, Amy typed in *They already saw,* and waited, nervously, her heart pounding, for quite a long moment before pressing SEND.

She had never initiated cybersex, not even in the stifling boredom of her North Carolina hotel room—it had always been Mike. That high-speed Internet connection—nine-ninety-five a day, highway frickin' robbery if you asked her—had pretty much been wasted.

She'd shot one blurry, off-kilter photo of her snatch with the digital camera she'd borrowed, and had emailed it to him from her room in the Raleigh Hilton only with the insistence that he delete it right away. (He hadn't—in fact, she'd discovered it on his hard drive months later—but then again, it could really be anybody's snatch, especially since she'd named the file "Internet download 12765" in the hopes that, if it did go astray, it could never be traced back to her.) For a technical writer, she was woefully behind the times.

Now, though, she could feel the heat in her low-riding, hip-hugging pants, could even feel the seam of the too-tight pair rubbing against her clit through the cherry-graced panties, grinding the cotton into her as she pressed her thighs together. She could feel her nipples hardening in her T-shirt and tried very hard to avoid thinking about how visible they were to the six German students discussing whether it was *Wie geht es dir* or *Wie geht es ihnen.*

This time, Mike's response was all but immediate. *Really. Do tell.*

You forgot to do laundry yesterday, she typed quickly, retreating into her bitchy voice in an attempt to banish the question she'd begged. She erased that message before sending, and felt the blood pounding in her temples as she typed quickly: *The German students are checking out my ass.*

This wasn't, strictly speaking, true, however high her cherry thong was riding in back. After all, she was sitting in a high-backed chair against a wall, and none of the *Geht es ihnen* crowd could see her waist, let alone the top of her thong.

But, actually, now that she thought about it, she had noticed one of the guys behind the counter looking when she'd gotten up to refill her coffee about ten minutes ago.

I bet u gave him a hard on, came Mike's response.

pROBABLY NOT, she typed irritably, not realizing she'd hit the CAPS LOCK key; when she backspaced to retype it, she pondered for a second and decided to play along. She glanced over her shoulder surreptitiously and then typed *I know I did. I saw it.*

There was a long pause, and Mike typed a simple *hot.*

Amy froze up, at a loss, not sure what to type next; Mike saved her from the decision by following up with something that all but handed her the next line.

That make you wet? he asked.

Amy didn't actually know the answer to that question, because the server getting a hard-on didn't make her wet at all—mostly because he hadn't, at least, not as far as she knew. But something about this whole weird situation, about knowing how much this turned Mike on, about pushing her own limits while she sat here pretending to work, made her jump in headfirst.

Yeah, she typed. *It made me incredibly wet.*

Your pussy is wet now, isn't it? answered Mike.

Had she been alone, Amy would have checked; she would have undone the top button of her low-riders, slid her hand down her tight pants and into her cherry-bearing thong, and felt her pussy to see if she was, in fact, as juicy as she thought she was. Now, though, that wasn't an option; ironically, it also wasn't necessary. She could feel the liquid heat between her legs and knew that the white cotton thong was soaked.

dripping, she typed, her hands shaking a little as she did.

cherries soaked, typed Mike.

y, was all she could manage with her hands shaking like that, but after typing it she did manage to backspace and type it as a capital letter. She took pleasure in using the annoying Internet shorthand, but not nearly as much pleasure as she took in admitting that her panties were drenched. It probably had nothing to do with the barista checking out her ass, whether he had or he hadn't. But it had plenty to do with Mike, sitting at home and taunting her. She found her hips moving almost imperceptibly, in a rhythm that matched the pounding of her heart, and every little squirm she gave rubbed the seam of her jeans against her clit, soaking the thong even more.

I like that, came Mike's response after a long time.

I bet you do, typed Amy, regaining her composure—and control of her fingers.

There was a long pause. Amy took deep breaths, glancing around to make sure that the German students and coffee servers weren't watching her. They weren't—in fact, they were completely ignoring her, as she might have expected—but she could feel her face getting flushed and she imagined, just for a second, that they all knew what she was doing. Every sordid detail. The thought sent a fresh surge of shivers through her body, and she fought to control them as she pressed her thighs together, rocking back and forth so subtly as to not show a thing—but still sending an ache to her clit as the seam of her tight pants rubbed against it.

Then the silence was broken; she heard the chime in her headphones that told her she had email—just as she got Mike's new IM.

Check your email and you'll see how much.

Amy's head spun, knowing what to expect. Her hands went all shaky again and hovered over the keyboard as she got ready to type *that is SO not a turn-on,* but before she could, she realized that, bizarrely, it was.

Amy was tucked into a corner, nobody and nothing behind her but a wall with a framed print of a cup of coffee and the morning paper.

But still she glanced over her shoulder, as if to make sure the cup of coffee couldn't see her, before she opened her email and saw the blurry, oversaturated picture of Mike's hard cock, his hand wrapped around the base as if holding it out for the camera—or her.

She had always thought it was *so* fucking tacky for guys to email pictures of their cocks. Not that she'd ever been emailed one—but just on principle. Totally stupid, clueless, idiotic male weirdness.

But this was Mike's hard-on, and she'd given it to him—just

by typing, sitting here and typing in a cafe while he stroked off at home. She felt a weird sense of pride, the way she did when he got hard at home, when they were making love, *before* they were making love—the rush that came from knowing she'd gotten him rock hard, and that he'd do anything to have her.

She typed her next line without thinking, her inner porn writer taking over as the pressure of her thighs gently surging together sent a fresh ache through her.

I can't go around flashing my underwear and making men get big fat hard-ons all day, she wrote. *I'd better go take them off.*

There was a long pause, as Amy struggled with herself—if Mike didn't give her just the right response, of course, she was going to abandon the game, forget about it; there was no way she was stripping her panties off in a coffee shop bathroom without at least a little encouragement.

But she knew already, without a doubt, that the encouragement would be forthcoming.

That'd make this one even harder, Mike wrote.

Then, *bra too, please,* he added, and Amy felt her nipples harden noticeably.

She probably would have done it without a thought if she'd been wearing a looser T-shirt, but laundry day had left her with one a size too small. The lines of her bra were already visible, and she knew that their absence would probably be noticed by the German students, and maybe even the cafe employees.

So, *bra too? really?* she typed, not sure whether she was hoping Mike would recant or she just wanted to hear it again—but, in a way she couldn't really admit, knowing the answer.

Really, Mike's message came back. *Please.*

Nervously, Amy stood up, turned her laptop slightly toward the wall to hide the screen from any prying eyes, and flashed one of the German students the look that café-goers all over the world recognize from the owners of laptops. "Ja, ja," he said, waving his hand to indicate he'd watch her computer while she used the restroom.

Amy's hands were shaking so hard she could hardly get the door locked. When she kicked off her shoes, she found the tile floor moist and icky, but it didn't give her pause the way it usually would. She slid her hands under the waistband of her thong, giving a silent and rueful glance to the silk-screened cherries. She pulled her soaked thong down, stepped out of it, and braced herself against the handicap bar as she eased her hand between her legs.

She was wet, all right—wetter than she had even suspected. She began to rub her clit. Her whole body flooded with pleasure. Fuck, she was close. She could do it right now, could almost come standing up. If she did want to come all she had to do was sit on the toilet for a second with her legs spread, rub her clit perhaps fifteen, twenty times—she'd come so hard she'd scream. She could go back and tell Mike about it. He'd like that.

But he'd like it better if she did it in front of her computer, with everyone watching, with no one—hopefully—knowing.

Amy stepped back into her jeans and tugged them into place. Now the seam that had so tormented her was raw, naked against her, her lips swollen and spread with arousal, her sensitive clit exposed. She quickly undid her bra and slid it out one armhole without removing her tight T-shirt. Her nipples, hard with arousal, showed plainly through the thin, sweat-damp cotton.

She balled up her bra and thong and tucked them into her front pocket. *Thank god I don't wear underwire*, she thought.

She splashed cold water on her face and left the bathroom. Returning to her table, she gave a nod to the German-speaking watchdog, feeling suddenly guilty that she was doing something so wrong right in front of him, and right in front of everyone.

The German student nodded at her—and she wondered, though she couldn't be sure, if she saw his eyes lingering a little bit over her chest, noting the difference.

Then she sat down, and she didn't care anymore.

With her panties gone, the seam of the tight jeans rubbed so hard against her clit as she leaned forward against the chair that she knew, then, that she was going to come for Mike. She was going to come hard, and it was going to take all of her willpower, every bit of her strength, to keep from crying out as she did so.

She took a deep, deep breath, slowly and carefully, before typing into the open IM window.

I'm back, she wrote.

Everything gone now? Mike typed back.

Panties and bra, she wrote.

Tight shirt. They can see your nipples.

This time she was sure. The German guy was definitely staring at her. She looked up at him with a fierce look, and he glanced away, reddening.

Yes, she typed. *They can.*

R U wet? typed Mike.

Amy leaned forward against the edge of the chair, her legs spread just enough to drive the seam of her jeans deep between her lips. It abraded her clit, almost painfully—but firmly enough that she knew she could do it, right here, the movements of her hips tiny and hidden by the table.

She had to take several deep breaths before she could type: *More than wet. I'm going to cum.*

She immediately flushed at the use of that stupid shorthand—it always annoyed her in porn, and about ten times more in cybersex, the little she'd had of it. But there she was using it, and somehow she wanted to type it again. So *I'm going to fucking cum,* she typed quickly, her hands flying suddenly sure and steady on the keyboard at one hundred words per minute. *I'm going to cum cum cum cum,* she typed, kind of weirded out that the stupid word turned her on. She barely even noticed her hips were moving, and she hoped the German students didn't notice at all.

Me 2, typed Mike, and Amy's response shocked even her.

Show me, she wrote.

Mike did. For a while all he typed was a series of undecipherable, random signifiers, which Amy figured meant he was having an orgasm. It all started with *AAAAAAAAAAAAAHHHHHHHH* and was followed rapidly by *aaasdfk;dfasjkl;sdfjk;lasdf j;kadfsjk;dfsajkl;dfas* and *mmmmmmmmmmmmmmmmmmmmmmmmmmmmmmmmmm* and a few other lines that almost made Amy lose her buzz. But then her email chimed, and she didn't even glance around before switching windows.

There it was—Mike's cock in midspurt, almost unrecognizable, a blurred stream of semen erupting from a huge pink blob, several droplets visible on the camera lens.

Then Amy understood the language of instant-message orgasm, slamming her hand on the keyboard and conjuring a string of random characters as her orgasm took her fiercely. She didn't notice or care what she got, but she felt obligated to let Mike know she was coming, and this was absolutely the best she could do.

Amy leaned forward hard against the chair and came, biting her lip the whole time. She shut her eyes like she was thinking so hard it hurt; then, as her orgasm pulsed through her and she realized that she'd just come in full view of everyone in the cafe, she nervously reached for her cell phone like she thought she was getting a call—a weird, reflexive sleight-of-hand trick so that it seemed she was doing something other than wanking in public, something other than coming as hard as she'd ever come in her life, looking at a digital picture of her boyfriend's cock while the business of the cafe went on around her.

mmmmmmmmmmmmmmmmmmmmmmmmmmmmmmmmmm flashed on the screen. Apparently Mike had gotten the message that she was coming, and responded with a basically incomprehensible message of his own. Even so, it served the purpose.

Amy took a deep breath, closed the picture of Mike's cock, and glanced at the German students, who were studiously ignoring her. She leaned back and nervously crossed her legs.

take the rest of the day off, Mike had typed.

Amy cleared her throat, glanced at the remains of her half-decaf latte.

Y, she typed, and closed her laptop.

METAMORPHOSIS

Anastasia Mavromatis

Does every girl undergo a phallic stage, experiencing envy? According to Freud, it occurred in early childhood. I can't recall craving cock until my late teens, when I creamed my way through Top of the Pops. Perhaps I've suppressed the earlier memories. As far as the story goes, a girl yearns to be like a boy, envying the flesh dangling between his legs. I didn't get it. I didn't envy Thomas or his cocktail wiener in kindergarten; he accidentally zipped his little sausage and bolted out of the toilets in tears. The other phenomenon that allegedly marks a girl's sexuality is her father, and I couldn't avoid rewinding to this theoretical blunder the moment my mother awoke.

She personified Clytemnestra, and it was my mission, as Electra, to annihilate her. Daddies infuse girls with their first impressions of the opposite sex, and mothers compete with daughters. The Electra complex spilled out and was the source of academic stag fights; Freud and Jung fought, diverged, and led separate lives. It didn't aid me. When I turned four, Dad paid the ferryman.

"Where's the coffee?" My mother rubbed her eyes and yawned. The hem of the heavy dressing gown caressed the tiles.

"At its usual spot."

"This is what I get each time I visit—attitude."

"You'll ask about your potential grandchildren next," I snapped.

It was standard practice: at five, I knew I'd have to marry my sweet prince, and that marriage would produce grandchildren. It was like a double major: marriage and children. She glanced at me, her fixed smile showing off her Hollywood dentures. Each tooth sparkled, gaining a ghoulish iridescence from the bleak London sky.

"You don't fuck that much, do you?"

Normally I would have yelled: "Mum, please!" or "Enough!" But I knew her better than my husband's dick. I lit up instead; being married to a stockbroker was as exciting as flossing my teeth on a Saturday night. "The love of money is the root of all evil"—and led to a stagnant sex life.

"Bloody hell," she waved at the air. "Don't you read the papers? It's all over the television. I thought you stopped. It'll kill you."

"It's none of your business if we fuck, or don't fuck." How could we fuck if we had you in our faces each weekend? Who was I kidding? The FTSE 100 Index seduced Michael.

"How are you going to have children? The stork?" Her scent of Tabu shrieked like a banshee.

"It's all over the news. I can have donated sperm or try IVF. Maybe a surrogate...Why do you wear that perfume?" I needed unadulterated fornication.

"That's awful, a surrogate...Michael shooting blanks?"

"Not your business."

She located my favorite black satin pajamas and managed

to charm Michael away from his dressing gown—for her rheumatism. The cashmere gown I had bought Michael caressed her bony shoulders each weekend. The sprightly woman stretched upward, complaining, "What happened to the coffee mug tree I bought you last Christmas?" I was wrestling the Freudian High Sea, waiting for the Flying Dutchman.

"I'm late."

"I come to visit, and you're off to work—on a Saturday?"

"I have the shop to manage."

"I don't understand. Michael has a good job. Where is he?"

Yes, he had a job, and I could focus on procreation, gestation, and shitty diapers. Then it would open the door to a Freudian catwalk, with my mother parading my pajamas as the babies brought up vomit and cried for tit.

"Watching football at the pub," I said. And I thought, she's in my face, dressed in my pajamas and Michael's dressing gown.

It was Freudian revenge: explain your mother's habits Missy, and when are you planning on putting a stop to it? I could picture the bearded psychiatrist smiling with glee, smoking his fat oral fixation.

"You colored your hair," she said, leaning closer. "Nice color. What is it?"

"Clairol."

"Nice. Which shade?"

"I forgot." I knew better. Fleet Street journalists would ransack trashcans; my mother would scour the bathroom for the box, and if that didn't work, she'd pretend she lost her three-carat sparkler and wade through the trash. She'd note the shade and dash to Boots. The girls at my store would titter and placate me with: How cute, Stace, she's trying to fit in. She'll get over it, Stace.

They didn't know about the pajama-gown fixation. I'd been

too busy to notice, but Michael, with his attention to detail and focus, decided to take a dump.

"You know I like your mother, but I don't know why she has to be here every weekend."

"Loneliness?"

"Try forgetfulness."

"What? She's not forgetful."

"She forgets to pack her nightie and gown—each time, and besides, it's fucking weird to see her wear the satin pajamas I bought you." The pajamas I'd paraded for him, the same pajamas that gave him a hard-on.

"I think you need to approach it gently, Stace, you don't want to offend her."

"Approach what?"

"She's taken to wearing my dressing gown."

"Your point being?" Miffed, I turned over, and switched off my lamp.

"Babe..." His fingers crept over my flannel-clad hip.

"I'm tired." Great. My mother infiltrated our bed.

It was as though she had stepped into my skin; my silk pajamas were a second skin to her, and I was left with my ragged Clash T-shirt. Michael's gown operated as an embrace: a psychotherapist's wet dream. My kundalini migrated to my brain, and each prickling ache highlighted my sex crisis.

"It's not as painful as women imagine. I'm piercing the hood. Not the clit."

Phew?

Up until now, Doctor Mueller had been the only stranger with an Access All Areas pass to my twat. I held my breath as Jake gently slid a cotton Q-tip under my flesh and became initiated to my inner sanctum. Unlike Mueller, Jake admired my pussy.

"Great clit hood. We'll go for the VCH."

Jake knew more about clits than Mueller or felt more comfortable discussing the variations of clit piercings. The VCH, or vertical clitoral hood piercing, offered ample pleasure; I'd definitely gone troppo.

"Four week healing time, could take an extra week. Depends on how well you look after it, follow my advice." I heard metal clanging and gazed up to see a pair of large, gloved hands.

"Sure it won't kill me?"

"Love, I do about twenty clits a day. I'm a pro," he said, cocking his head to one side, revealing a multicolored phoenix on his neck.

"What if the piercing makes it all...you know?"

"I use a needle receiving tube. No freehand bullshit. Your sex life is gonna rock after this."

"All right...do it." I squeezed my eyelids shut.

The level of stimulation depended on the jewelry. It was something I hadn't read in high school, and according to Jake, "made experimentation fun." I'd allow four weeks to pass, and see how it worked: Ring or banana bar? I could vary the weight and style, and see how my excitement varied. If only Freud were here to see this!

"Now there's no point pricking you only to prick you," Jake said, and with that I almost lost my breath. I remembered my next Pap smear at Mueller's. How would he react? Jarred by a prick of the surgical kind, I opened my lips to dissuade Jake.

It was over in less than ten seconds.

"Is that it?"

Oooh shit!

"You expecting microsurgery, love?"

"I've got a gyno appointment next week," I said, propping myself up on my elbows. Jake inspected the piercing, his eyes magnified a hundredfold behind his bifocals.

"It'll be fine...oh, that? Doctors see everything anyway."

"But Dr. Mueller, he's so...vintage."

"It'll give the geezer some excitement," Jake winked. "You're ready to roll. Now remember..."

He explained the rigorous healing routine. It was as simple as brushing my teeth: bathe the piercing twice a day, preferably under running water, with an antibacterial.

"And don't pick at it."

"No offense, Jake, but I don't want to look at it right now."

"You'll be thanking me, girl."

I needed a S.W.A.T. team to monitor the perimeter each weekend and keep my mother out. The poor old dear would crumble at the notion of me having my crumpet pierced, and Michael? I had no idea about his leanings; he had no secret porn stash, and I checked his Internet histories, to flounder in a state of perpetual melancholy. Work became his life; rising share prices warmed his insides.

Michael trotted off to bed shortly after my return, and my mother offered to make cocoa. The tingling itch between my legs decided to go for a gallop. I needed to scratch it. I crossed and uncrossed my legs.

"Are you all right? You look strange. Twitchy."

"I'm fine, Mum."

"Did you argue with Michael?"

"How could I? I wasn't home."

"On your portable phone."

"I didn't call him, and it's called a cell or mobile phone."

"He was arguing with someone..." Her eyes narrowed. She lowered her voice and leaned forward. "You've got to keep an eye on him, love. He's a man...and that argument..."

"I don't want to hear it, really. Stop it."

"It wasn't a normal argument. That's all I'm saying."

I gazed at my satin pajamas. Normal? Was there such a thing?

I would have asked her, but my clit needed a cool, sensual bath.

Pride swelled within my clit. I turned the piercing twice daily, and four weeks later, ended the trial period in a sweaty orgasmic canter. I made good; my pussy erupted like a geyser after I gave it a going over with a swish clit vibrator. Triumphant, I stepped out of the shower—hoping for seconds, possibly thirds.

"Stace..."

I grabbed the nearest towel, salivating for a quick slap and fuck.

"Yes?"

"Have you seen my emerald tie? The one your mother bought?"

"She bought that a year ago."

"I've a meeting."

He opened the door as I had one foot on the bath edge and my butt in the air. His eyes didn't roam or make an anal detour.

"Good luck...can't help you with your tie."

"Thanks."

I stepped into his dressing gown and followed him to our bedroom.

"Can't find my tie. Are you sure you haven't seen it?"

It's on a VIP trip to the rubbish dump.

I didn't confess my sin. I lay on the bed, strategically parting the dressing gown. I was ready to unveil my bejeweled clit.

"Michael?" I purred.

"I'm running late."

He settled for cerise and tightened the knot. Michael briefly evaluated his ensemble in the mirror, and his eyes avoided Queen Kitty throughout my slag overture.

"You remind me of your mother in my dressing gown," he said.

He bent down, kissed me on the cheek, and smiled.

"Not a grand appetizer I'm afraid. No offense, Stace."

I sat, a stunned mullet.

"I'll be home after nine tonight."

My mother's words circled my thoughts like ravenous condors; you're not giving him enough attention.

"Hey! Get back here!" I pushed myself up, my Mediterranean temper bubbling under the surface, and entered the hall as the front door clicked shut. "Fuck you..." My verve shriveled to a hoarse whisper.

The day progressed. I achieved the first of two objectives. I dumped my mother's favorite sleep ensemble at the charity shop on Bloomsbury Street. Margot and Rod, the genteel store managers, thought I'd made an error.

"Divorce," I said, desperate for a quick exit; the shop pulsed with Eau de Geriatric and stale sweat.

"Oh," they nodded, their solemnity as false as my Dior pout.

I reached my second objective in Soho where I'd kept my hair appointment. Claire inspected my hair. Her physique, leathers, and blue-black ass unnerved me. Her lofty heels added two inches, making her six foot two.

"Claire? I put a client on hold, and I can't seem to...get them back?" The harried receptionist feebly smiled.

"One tick, love," the urban Amazon said, sauntering to the counter. Her leather-clad thighs confirmed arduous climbs, cycles, and intense sex. I watched her slink toward the receptionist. Thou shalt not covet another woman's ass. It had been six months, and three days since I'd envied a woman's derriere at my local health club, and I had no one to confess my sins to. I'd gladly confess all to Claire.

I sat, observing the impasse between Claire and her temp. Claire wagged her finger, and the girl nervously nodded:

"How many times already? It's a phone with a hold button, innit?"

"S-sorry, Claire."

The salon expanded at that instant. I felt alone, and stood out like a suppurating ass boil in a black gown that resembled a king-sized napkin. Clients chatted to stylists, colorists poured over swatches, offering sage advice, and I stared at the reflection before me thinking, I am not going to resemble my mother.

"Back. Now…why are you cutting all this hair? It's lovely." She faced the mirror and waited for a valid reason. I inwardly noted her tone; *innit* wasn't my favorite chav slang of the year, but Claire's tangy-sweet voice handled it well. Her pallor worked with her scarlet lip stain, and the motion of her lips riveted me to the chair. It would have been forward or loopy to tell her that I resembled my mother and how this collided with my libido.

"I need a change."

"The relationship change."

"Come again?"

"I see it all the time."

"How long do you give me?"

She laughed, running her fingers though my hair.

"A shame to cut. Must've taken years to grow."

Had I been a celebrity, I could have earned a few profile points for this abrupt change.

"Cut it."

"You're married," she craned her neck. "That's a spiffy ring."

The ring that binds; at this point I would have slept with Lord Sauron.

"I want something new. Revolutionary. I wouldn't mind a few blood red highlights in the front…something that would make everyone sit up and take notice"—and shut my mother's mouth once and for all.

"There's only so much a hairdo can do. Are you sure? Did you want something like this?" She twirled her hair round her finger.

"More positive than a pregnancy test."

"You're not pregnant are you? Some of the pigments and chemicals are…"

"No." I'd need to book an appointment in advance, lest I mucked up Michael's bullish stock highs.

Claire donned an apron and decided to wash my hair. My contentment surpassed that of a small kitten. She massaged my scalp, ironing out my mental knots. I crossed my legs tightly, appreciating the ululating frisson of steel against clit. The jolt settled to a warm ripple. It infiltrated my inner thighs and tickled my skin receptors. Each receptor spawned microscopic fingers that taunted my nerves. Claire opened her mouth, and my brain went on involuntary mute. I filtered out my ego, to make way for the sex-starved id.

I returned to the salon over the course of three weeks as a volunteer; my girls believed my lies: Mum holidaying in France and Michael working overtime. The reality, of Michael loathing my shorn locks and Mum ransacking my wardrobes for pajamas, propelled me forward. I spent the time training Claire's hapless receptionist on the art of phone manners, all the while watching my quarry. Claire traipsed the salon, displaying her smile, ass, and cockney spiked aura. My wish arrived on the third week. I accepted Claire's invitation for a quick drink at her local.

New faces turned our way.

"Never mind those tossers." Claire winked and sought the bar. "You can have what I'm having. No pints."

"Okay...sure."

"Get a table."

Our quiet drinks began thus. She returned with two cosmopolitans. The boys to our right cast discreet glances in our direction, and Claire didn't have to pretend; she wasn't interested. The football match continued. A faraway group of bedraggled office receptionists groaned, and a triumphant cheer filled my head. Arsenal was winning, and that's all I cared about—Michael would be spewing nails, losing bets, and tearing his hair out.

"You're with the fairies. Don't tell me...you're a secret Arsenal fan." Her dazzling green eyes stopped on my mouth.

"How did you guess?"

She leaned forward, and brought her finger to her plump lips.

"Don't let that cat out, we'll have a shit storm." Claire giggled, covering my hands with hers. "I think it's time for another."

"My turn." It was only fair to reciprocate.

One become two, and two became three. At some point we entered the exponential scale. The pub faded, and the surrounding men and women became a blur. Their significance reduced as Claire's tactile fingers slid past my wrists. The warmth blurred the pub patrons and oscillated between our bodies. Her thumbs circled my flesh, prying open my thoughts.

"Your hair looks great," she said, her eyes glimmering. "Tell me about the change."

Effortless. The spell had been cast the moment I entered the salon. This lucidity unshackled my repressed body. Claire slipped her knee between my legs, and the texture of warmed leather eradicated Michael. It all tumbled out: the nightwear, my mother's habits, and Michael's immunity to my asshole. Claire's eyes absorbed my words.

"She copies me," I said, dazed by my revelation.

"It's a little creepy."

"A little?"

I'd summarize my life before this moment as stasis. Life grew stubby legs and crept by like a fat Dachshund; I stood like a figurine, unable to grasp anything solid. I wore my mother's mask, or she quietly fitted me out over the years.

"Sounds like you've dealt with the bulk. Can I call you Frau Freud?"

"No," I wanted a meatier portion, something rude and vulgar—Frau Fuck.

Claire's fingers tapped my flesh, and my legs applied pressure to her thigh.

"I know what you want," I said, perked up by our sixth drink.

"If you're aware, and you've remained calm, then you're up for it too," she said, releasing her hold.

"You're into psych babble. Freud?"

"A bit of everything, I'm afraid. I'm an intellectual slut," she offered her Jungian challenge, briefly explaining his view of societies, one's place within them, and the roles one played. "You can't be both a politician and poet. You'd be doubted. You can't be an English lit professor and Angus Young or you'd be a dilettante."

Her pronunciation of dilettante pumped extra joules into my clit; it hummed beneath its hood. The shiny pink tip of her tongue caressed the corner of her mouth.

"Which are you?" Her lips formed a perfect circle. I blinked, expecting a stream of smoke to caress my face. One blink, two…

"I'm a horny slag on the inside." I lived for an unregimented fuck.

"And?"

"A shopkeeper by day?" I laughed, downing another mouthful. "I couldn't tell you about the other side."

"Try."

She didn't break her gaze. Her knee inched farther, to rest against my panties. I was beyond reclaiming my words. Her knee worked my cunt with firm circular strokes, tenderizing my flesh, and giving new meaning to uniform circular motion. I didn't hold on to finite sexual nomenclature or the "I'm not lesbian, but," view. Anything was possible. Life didn't take customized orders. My pussy wept: elation, anticipation, and need wrestled for supremacy. I succumbed to my burning labia and pressed my cunt against her knee.

"I don't know…that's the bitch of torment," I said. "Don't stop…fuck..."

That inner bitch began scratching from within. She clawed at my throat, eager to escape. A star exploded in my head. It could have been the alcohol, but I knew better. She was I, I was Claire ,and my inner tormenter needed to climb out of the maternal square, rip away the apron strings, and go to town in the flimsiest dress sans panties.

My heart beat like a tribal drum; heartily, each resonant thud relayed blood to my pelvis. I couldn't recall Claire's first caress away from the pub or pinpoint the instant our lips touched. We took the Tube, silently staring at each other throughout our journey to her Bayswater flat. We fell, shortly after stumbling through her threshold. Our synergy felt natural or arranged by a higher power. Her lips paired with mine, and we fluttered. Her hands gleefully squeezed my breasts. We then hit the floor, our lips straining for an extra sip. Our teeth met briefly, and my legs gripped her hips, pulling her closer. The guilty cloud above was lined with quicksilver that dripped into my head, infusing me with febrile cravings that roused a frenzy of ravenous urges that resonated through my head, to leave me swaying like a dervish.

Claire unbuttoned my shirt and tore off my bra. I watched my tits jiggle. She ground her hips against mine, riveting me to the hardwood floor. I watched her mouth feast; each hypnotic roll of her tongue frittered away my memory. I couldn't recall my clothes or what became of them.

"Bite me," I instructed. Her eyes rolled up, and her mouth tenaciously clung to my prickling nipple. I swallowed, gripping her tighter, my thighs contracting and relaxing. My panties reached their maximum absorption. Claire bared her teeth, and nipped each nipple. Left, right, left...

My clit pulsed to her tugging front teeth. She clamped, and I squeezed, my limbs shivering as sparks ignited my insides. My clit rode the tempest until I heaved, and my spinal column absorbed the swift fiery current.

"I'm a fucking mess..."

"You're a running fountain..." she said, her face nestled between my legs. There were no butterfly kisses along my midriff or sugarcoated murmurs; the crow flew a straight line, demanding sweat infused flesh.

Claire pulled my panties. Her relentless fingernails scored my thighs on their descent. I jiggled and writhed, thighs taut with anticipation and need.

"Just...c'mon." I thrust my bejeweled pussy in her face and remembered Jake.

You'll remember me, girl.

Her tongue could have been a guitar pick. It parted my labia, plucking musky notes. It swished and sashayed over my clit, to apply pressure. I grunted, and Claire's leaden breath revealed her libidinous depths. Her tongue tormented my clit, bumping my piercing until a hot steak of lust tore through my stomach. Her sticky lips stepped in, tugging my clit bar.

"How pretty." She raised her chin and ran her index finger over her mouth. Pussy gloss coated her lips; she deposited my arousal into her mouth and sucked her finger dry.

"God, yes," I whispered, craving her stiff chocolate-brown nipples.

"It's time to lick you all the way home."

Her tongue bore down until the faint pulse in my clit shattered my thoughts. I gripped her head, hips spiraling beyond my natural control. I jerked this way and that, bathing her mouth and chin—freshly squeezed. I couldn't lose my momentum or I'd shrivel and stutter like a frazzled brat.

"Get up now," I ordered, abandoning my patience. My hands gripped her upper arms, and I heaved. "Hands against the... wall." I unzipped her pants and tugged until she had nothing to hide. The leather held her knees in place. I pushed her arm away until our tits rubbed, and I awoke to their texture, pinching and tweaking them at will.

"Open." It wasn't a request; there were no pretty pleases, with sugar on top. I pulled back her hair, rejoicing at the texture of her nipples bumping against my chest, and dove in, tasting the remnants of my arousal and orgasm. I owned her mouth, I thought. I released her, nipping her plumped lower lip.

"Do whatever you want—"

"Shhh...over there." I pointed toward her sofa, and watched her crawl, her ripe ass in the air, leather pants hobbling her to a rustling shuffle. She whimpered a little. A mock protest, perhaps? I didn't care. I positioned her over the sofa and parted her thighs.

"I like it like this. You can't run," I said, not that she needed to flee. I acted on my own instinct. Every salty rivulet of sweat coalesced, forming a slick coat along her spine. I licked slowly, breathing in her scent until my stomach expanded. The urge to burst, litter the flat with my slippery insides, painted lurid scenes over my beige stained life.

"It's so sweet," I whispered, glancing at her buttocks.

"I can't wait...c'mon, Stace..."

My tongue collapsed at her lumbar region, and I closed my eyes, savoring the salty tang of her perspiration. I squeezed her right buttock until she expelled a heady sigh. Then I made for my heinous descent, nipping her buttocks with my teeth.

"Lick it...lick it now."

I pinched, kissed, and slapped her trembling ass, until she blushed rose. Only then could I retreat, and anoint my fingers with her slick cream. My three fingers burrowed deep. They twisted, and Claire shouted my name repeatedly. My other hand pressed against her stomach, pulling her into my riptide, while I curled against her G-spot. My mantra continued; *Fucking you is fucking me over, and I like being fucked. I need it. Badly.* This thought gained lucidity as Claire's visceral cries rose in pitch. She infiltrated the furniture and penetrated my skin. I squeezed my thighs together, jamming my three fingers into Claire's snug hole, until her G-spot took her over the limit, and we lost our heads.

Regaining breath, I grasped her hair and turned her around. My lips forced hers apart; I dived in, ransacking her tender mouth until I needed a fresh gasp of air.

"Knees sore or can you do with some more?"

I had it planned; she'd kneel over my face, thighs parted

wide, and I'd suck her off on my back. I then beheld a beautiful butterfly on her damp naked mound. I knew the genus by heart: Odysseus. The tattooist's shading animated the vivid blue butterfly. It could have taken flight at any second.

"Did that hurt?" My finger traced each wing.

Claire rubbed her ass. "You gain pleasure from pain. Wouldn't you agree?" Her eyes danced over my clit. "I need another helping. No one waiting up for you?" Claire gripped my shoulders until I winced. Her tender ass met the floor, and she reclined, her inner thighs tensing with renewed anticipation.

"They can wait," I said, and allowed her hands to guide my face to her radiant cunt; my lips prickled, and I opened wide, my thoughts as light as dandelion seeds in the breeze.

NEW YORK PEEP SHOW

Virgie Tovar

More than a few breast men have told me about the famed peep shows on Eighth Avenue, back before Giuliani cleaned up midtown Manhattan. They recount the hours and twenty-dollar bills spent on the anonymous women—some even lactating—who stood behind a wall and offered their breasts through a window to all who were interested in a few minutes of groping.

I've been to plenty of strip clubs and peep shows, but I had never seen a place like this one.

I was visiting New York City. I used to live close to the seedy part of town and so I'd spent my fair share of time in the porn stores of Eighth. This place, however, I had never come across. I walked inside with a guy friend who happened to have aspirations of fucking me. We walked through the place, exchanging smiles as we passed ridiculous porn titles. It was small and smelled like bleach and incense. I was wearing a short red dress with a thin, shiny, black belt that cinched me just below my breasts. My high heels were shiny like the belt, and my legs were bare. The dress was too small for my full double-Ds and compressed my chest. It was only by the mercy of the low swooping neckline that I could zip it up at all. My boobs were squeezed tightly together; the unforgiving and insufficient material forced my tits to bulge out of the top, allowing any curious eye to feast on the globular tops and cleavage. I had on my new orange blossom perfume and my hair was down. We walked everywhere in the front area and then to the back area labeled BOOTHS. When we got back there we were greeted by a line of men.

We got in the back of the line and I was dying with curiosity. I tried to see what was awaiting us at the front of the line by getting up on my tiptoes but couldn't figure it out. The men in the line in front of me kept turning around and looking at me, their eyes scanning my breasts. One even looked at my companion and said, "You need to get her inside that booth." When we were third from the front, I finally saw what it was. At the front of the line, a man in his twenties stood waiting with a ten-dollar bill in his hand. He had a couple of friends with him and they were encouraging him to slip the bill into a small slot.

He walked up tentatively and slid it in. A window opened and then a few seconds later a pair of huge tits popped through the window. I had only seen tits like those in movies. I guessed that they were at least an F-cup. He walked up, his back to the line, and began fondling them. Everyone could hear the woman behind the wall moaning. The friends were cheering as he pulled and twisted her prominent nipples and squeezed her round tits, his hands dwarfed. The ten dollars bought him about three minutes and then it was time for the next guy.

The show got me so fucking hot that I had to excuse myself, and I lost my place in line. I was warm and I walked around the front of the store, eyeing the selection they had in the "gonzo" section. My friend came around and asked me, whispering in my ear, if I'd gotten too turned on back there. His advances had been getting annoying, but I had indeed gotten too turned on back there, and I liked his mouth so close to my ear. I giggled and he asked if I wished I was that girl. I bit my lip and hit him in the shoulder. "Oh, really?" He knew exactly what my response meant. "Wait here. I'll be right back." He walked over to the counter and talked to the clerk. They looked at me and the clerk laughed, shaking his head. My friend extended his hand to the guy behind the counter. He looked in his palm and sighed. Before I knew it, he was leading me and Dave to the back area.

He led us into a narrow door and down a corridor. We stopped and there she was. All I saw was her back, but I knew it was her. The sides of her tits were visible from behind. All she had on was a little pair of tight black G-string panties, and her lower body swayed back and forth. Her feet (in scuffed pink heels) danced a little the way that mine do when I'm getting turned on while standing up. When the window closed, she stepped back and sat down. Her tits looked so heavy on her small frame. Her areolas were small, and her nipples were deliciously pert from all the fondling. She smiled at me and Dave.

The man from behind the counter spoke to her in Spanish and told her that she could take a fifteen-minute break. She looked at me and winked. *"Buena suerte, mija,"* (*Good luck, my girl*), she said as she walked past me, her shoulder sweeping mine. I turned around and asked her how big her breasts were. "Thirty-four double-F," she said. She trotted out, her tits swaying from side to side as she disappeared.

I walked over to the space where she had just stood. The small window was already open, a twenty-dollar bill being waved inside. I took it between two of my fingers and slid the larger window open. I unzipped my dress just enough to be able to maneuver my tits out. Then came the red bra. I was wearing the only bra I owned that clasped in the front. I unhooked it and my breasts came down a tiny bit to their natural resting spot. They were perky for their size: 40DD with big areolas and pert, chubby nipples. The guy on the other side reached inside and began to squeeze them. His thumbs went straight for my nipples, rubbing small circles as blood began to flow to them, filling them and making them more erect.

He massaged my tits and bounced them, grabbed my nipples like radio dials and tugged them. I could hear his breath getting louder and more labored. "How much to let me suck those big, beautiful titties?" he asked through the small window. I giggled and looked over at my friend. He smiled and mouthed "Fifty." I told him the amount and he tried to haggle over the price. I told him to get out of there if he was going to be a baby about it. Either he wanted to suck or he didn't. He relented, sliding a crisp fifty into the slot. I pushed them out, and his mouth was right there waiting. He grabbed my tits in his hands and took the firm nipple between his lips.

Dave moved in behind me and lifted my dress slightly. I looked back at him as his face moved into mine. I reached my hands behind me meekly and tried to push him away. He knew I didn't mean it. His lips grazed mine as his fingers made their way to my panties. He pushed his fingertips against the satin covering my slit as I spread my thighs and arched my back. He slid them up further to my clit and he began to rub his thumb against my hole and his index finger against my clit.

His mouth had made its way to my neck as the guy on the other side of the wall began sucking and biting my tits eagerly. My pussy was sopping wet and I could hear his finger playing with my juice. He pulled my panties up forcefully into the crack of my ass and the slit of my pussy, giving my sensitive virgin asshole and my erect clitty a jolt. He held my panties and jiggled them back and forth as he swatted my ass. Then he pulled them to the side roughly as his teeth bit into my neck.

I moaned as two of his fingers slid easily into my tight little pussy. He grabbed my ass and spread my cheeks, slipping another finger against my puckered asshole, pulling my dress down my shoulders. My tits were still on the other side of the wall when he lifted my dress completely over my ass and unzipped his pants. He grabbed my hair as he pulled his cock out. He told me to look at what I had done to him, how long I had made him wait. He reached into his pants and pulled out his erection, so stiff it pushed against his lower tummy. He pushed it up against my asshole as his hands made their way to the undersides of my breasts.

The guy on the other end had to have felt it when Dave entered me. Dave let the head slide from my asshole to my wet, ready snatch. I whispered that I wouldn't do it without a condom as he slid it into me in one long stroke. I moaned as he wrapped my hair around his fist so he could look over my shoulder at my tits and nipple deep inside the mouth of the guy on the other side of the wall. "I bet it's an old pervert sucking your big, beautiful young tits. I bet he has kids, a wife, but all he wants are those big juggs in his face. I bet the guy after him is a fucking fat pig who wants to suck your big titties dry. But you like that don't you, you slut?" The combination of the deep penetration, the mouth on my tits, and the dirty words in my ear were driving me fucking crazy.

All of a sudden I felt another mouth on my tits. Two mouths, one on each nipple, and Dave was still sliding his dick all the way in and all the way out, thrusting deep into my pussy as he teased my asshole. "Yeah, you like the dick of one guy in your pussy while another guy's mouth is on your pretty tits, huh?" He kissed my mouth when he wasn't talking. I could hear his dick going in and out, it was so wet. He grabbed my knee, holding it up and making my pussy so open as he pushed into me. I wasn't sure who was sucking on my tits at this point and I didn't care. It felt so good. There were teeth around my right nipple and a quick, talented tongue on the other. Dave's cock was so good and firm.

He released my knee, bending me over while he kept that prick inside. His balls were slapping against my skin as he held my hips. "Your slutty tail is gonna make me come, baby. You're fucking hot tight pussy is gonna make me blow my wad in you." He started to come. He pushed his cock in and out of me, alternately squirting in my pussy and on my asshole. He pulled me away from the window, my tits popping out of the anonymous mouths, so I could lick up the excess juice on his dick. He spanked my tits as I lapped it up.

After twenty minutes, the regular woman came back to her post. Dave had slid my panties and dress back to their original positions.

We left, smiling, and took a cab back to his apartment in Morningside Heights.

PHILOSOPHY CLASS

Tamara Rogers

He calls her dorm room at 11:00 P.M. at night, when her roommate is out. They've only been seeing each other for a week, and they've barely talked on the phone at all. But she recognizes him—who else would open with such a line?

"What are you wearing?" His tone is low, almost a whisper, a growl. Seductive. Sexy. It makes her wet right away.

She smiles, takes her Diet Coke, and sits down on the lumpy single bed. "Panties and a tank top," she says. "I was about to put my sweats on."

"Don't," he says. "What kind of panties?"

"A thong," she says. "White cotton."

"Is it nice and wet? Nasty?"

"Yeah," she coos. "It's soaked. I've been thinking about you all day."

"Can you see your tits through the tank top?"

"Yeah," she says. "You can see right through it."

"You've got the greatest tits," he says. "Nice and big."

She puzzles over that for an instant, glancing down at her A-cup breasts, but what the hell, this is phone sex, right? She runs her fingertips over her erect nipples and sighs, "You like my tits, huh?"

"Yeah," he says. "I love them. I'd love to do nasty things to them. Real nasty."

"Like what?" she asks.

"Slide my cock between them. Tit-fuck you."

"Wow," she says, a little surprised. This doesn't sound like him at all. He's never talked to her like this. Of course, they haven't been together long, but it still surprises her.

"Come on your face," he says. "Fuck your tits and come on your face. Would you like that?"

The nasty talk sends an unexpected surge through her body. She's really wet now, and she slides her hand into her thong and starts stroking her pussy, rubbing her firm clit and feeling how juicy she's getting.

"Yeah," she says. "No one's ever done that to me before."

"No one's ever come on that pretty face? Not even when you were sucking their cock?"

"Nah," she says, pressing hard on her clit so that she gasps a little. "I...always...swallow."

"Oh, yeah," he moans. "I love it when you swallow. Swallow my come after sucking my cock. If I was there what would you do?"

She can feel her clit throbbing against her fingers as she rubs it. "Take my panties off," she says. "Strip you naked. Sit on your face and suck your cock at the same time."

"Oh, yeah," he sighs, his voice low again. "I'd slip my tongue into your pussy, lick your clit. Are you good and wet?"

"Yeah," she says, her finger making little circles on her clit as she tucks the phone between her ear and shoulder. "I'm gushing." She starts to struggle out of her thong, tossing it on the floor next to her bed. She spreads her legs very wide, exposing her pussy, and starts to rub her clit faster.

"Mmm. Your juice would run all down my face. I'd lick it all up. What would you do with my cock?"

She's right on the edge now; she's never had phone sex, never even talked this nasty in person. She moans: "I'd run my mouth all over it. I'd suck it. I'd lick the head."

"Suck my come right off it?"

"Yeah," she sighs. "I'd suck your come."

"What then?"

She feels her mind swirling awkwardly after the images as she mounts closer and closer to her orgasm. "Oh, when I had you good and hard I'd turn around and sit down on your cock."

"Oh, yeah," he groans. "Slide it right into your pussy. Your nice wet pussy."

"Yeah," she whispers. "I'd fuck you so hard."

"Just like you did last night," he says.

She puzzles again. They didn't see each other last night. In fact, it's been three nights since they had sex. But she kind of goes with the flow, feeling her clit swelling as she gets closer. She's tottering on the edge, almost ready to come. Her mind rebels, wanting her to stop. Instead, she answers.

"Yeah," she moans. "Just like last night. Tell me how you fucked me last night."

"You got on top of me and pounded my cock into your pussy," he says. "Then I rolled you over and fucked you doggy-style. You slammed back onto me. Your pussy onto my cock. I fucked you so fucking hard—"

He lets out a groan and that's what drives her over the edge, both of them coming as the phone crackles with the volume of their passion.

As her orgasm fades away, she listens to the panting on the other end of the phone, and she starts to wonder about last night.

"Tommy?"

"Huh?"

"Is this Tommy?"

"Karen?"

Her heart races. She feels her face flushing hot, her pulse pounding in her ears.

"This isn't Tommy, is it?" she says.

"This isn't Karen?"

"Karen Hedley?"

"Yeah," he says. "This isn't...who is this?"

She shuts her eyes very tight and groans, a very different groan than the ones she issued moments ago.

"Karen Hedley's in B Dorm," she says nervously. "The numbers start with four-seven-four."

"Oh, shit," he says. "Not four-seven-five?"

"No. I get her calls all the time."

"No kidding."

"Who is this?"

"Oh, man," he says. "I'm really sorry. I thought you were Karen. I'm really, really sorry."

"Who is this?"

"Shit, I knew I recognized your voice! You're in my philosophy class. You asked the question about Sartre today. I had the comment about Camus."

No wonder the guy's voice sounds familiar. She remembers him talking in class; he sat right behind her.

Actually, as she recalls, he's kind of cute.

She clears her throat. "Look, um." She pauses. "Let's just pretend this never happened."

"You won't tell Karen?"

"It never happened," she says crisply.

"Um, okay. What's your name?"

"Never mind," she says. "It never happened."

"Um. Okay. Um, whoever you are?"

"Yeah?"

"Thanks," he says.

"Don't mention it," she says. He doesn't hang up. There's an awkward and very weird moment of silence.

Then, surprising herself, she says: "See you in philosophy class," and hangs up before he can say anything.

BLUE COCK

Maddy Stuart

He wanted me to take charge. I wasn't sure I'd be able to muster the venom and authority he wanted from me.

I had a few stock phrases lifted from pornography—"Suck my cock, you slut," and the rest of it—but I wondered if those worn clichés would have any power over him. He was a man who'd fucked men and women and professionals; who'd been on both the business and consumption ends of every toy imaginable; who'd seduced me into his strap-on fantasy by calling me "dearest" and "kitten" and taking me out to dinner. He was the veteran and I was the blushing neophyte, and I didn't trust the curved blue lump of plastic and mess of black straps he'd sent me in the mail ("Your cock, darling,") to prop up my wavering voice and unsteady hands.

I hadn't wanted him to come to my apartment. It was an embarrassment of lazy girlishness—flowery art nouveau posters curling at the corners, unread poetry books, a plump cat. He hadn't wanted me in his place either, which he shared with another man and a woman. So we'd split the cost of a hotel room downtown. There would be nothing there to reveal us to each other or to anyone else, something I suspected gave me much more relief than it did him.

I wanted to go up to the room first, alone, to get my bearings. The room had two twin beds, a smirk of innocence in a room so blank and seedy that it dripped with sex. I imagined the grunting of the businessmen on vacation from their wives, the wives on vacation from their children, the teenagers dreading their parents' phone calls. Probably they'd all raised an eyebrow at the sight of two twin beds.

I unpacked the necessary gear from my free-gift tote bag and spread it over the desk in the corner. Dildo, condom, lube, red lipstick. I had some water from a glass wrapped in plastic, then slipped off my winter coat and suit jacket and admired the tops of my breasts peeking out from under my camisole. The rest of the clothes I'd remove later. I tried to imagine myself a seductress, summoning pretty young men to my lair and doing unspeakable things to them. I texted him my room number and waited.

He would be leaning against the railing next to his bicycle when he received it, I imagined, with his hands in his pockets. His stomach would contract and his breathing would shorten. His cock, of course, would spring to life, begging to be touched. He'd take a moment to let everything settle, and then he'd pull open the lobby doors, resisting the urge to skip the elevator and sprint up the stairs three at a time.

While imagining the finer points of his movements, I heard a knock on the door and went to let him in. He greeted me, and I couldn't tell from his face if he was nervous or elated.

There was no sofa to sit on, so we sat slumped side by side on one of the tightly made beds. We'd been chatting for an hour in the coffee shop (where he'd completely dominated the conversation) before I'd made my way to the room, and there was nothing to do but begin. He expected me to do the work of beginning, so I gathered the harness and the dildo from the table, excused myself to the bathroom, and closed the door behind me.

I was supposed to emerge transformed and ready, but the toys didn't look as though they'd be enough for the metamorphosis. Once the straps were secured around my thighs, and the dildo wedged into place, it stuck out at right angles to my thighs and belly. I slid a condom on, remembering my high school health class instructions and pinching the tip. He'd told me he wanted me to wear the strap-on under my clothes, but I didn't understand how that could be possible. The mechanics of fitting it under jeans or a skirt were completely mysterious to me, so I settled for leaving my legs bare and slipping off my bra so my nipples would poke through the camisole. I smeared on my red lipstick in broad strokes, then turned the doorknob and stepped out of the bathroom with as much confidence as I could muster.

He was lying on the bed, still fully clothed. His face showed no response, no reaction to my emergence as a cock-bearing tigress. I was annoyed—he could at least give me the courtesy of telling me how hot I looked, how beautiful my cock was. But there was nothing. *In the coffee shop you didn't let me get a word in edgewise*, I thought, unnerved by the silence. After climbing into the bed beside him there was nothing to do but reach over, touch him, begin.

I leaned over and put my hand in his hair. It was dyed a bright and brassy blond, roots a mousy brown, and it was soft, softer than mine. I ran my fingers through it again and again, wondering why he dyed it and why he'd chosen that color. I savored the feel of it against my fingers, and moments later

I couldn't imagine why I had thought it would be difficult to begin. I unbuttoned his collared shirt all the way to the bottom and ran my hand across his exposed chest. His skin was smooth and hairless and completely unblemished, and he pushed his chest out for me like a man in a magazine

"Do you wax?" I asked him, my fingers tracing circles around his navel.

"No," he said. "I'm naturally hairless." His voice was quiet and hesitant. I considered the hair dye and the fashionable clothing, and decided not to believe him. He was a waxer.

I pulled his shirt away from his arms, guiding him to roll over onto his stomach. It was then that I had the full view of his shoulders, broad and sculpted, the blades gently rising from his back. He was a man fully committed to his own beauty, and it was pliable beneath my admiring hands.

The blue dildo sat nestled between my thighs, a dead thing wearing a condom, prodding him occasionally in ways I didn't intend or control. The time had come to put it to use.

"Do you want to suck me?" I asked him, and rose to my knees.

He didn't answer me, but turned over in bed and propped himself up with his elbow, taking the dildo in his free hand and guiding it into his mouth.

He pleasured the knob of silicone with more force and enthusiasm than the women in the fifteen-second porn movie clips I'd sought out late at night. His blond head bounced back and forth and his supporting arm appeared to strain, but of course I could feel nothing, couldn't even tell how deep he was going. It was a little like watching him doing it to someone else. Still, I didn't expect to be moved the way I was by the sight of him straining and toiling at my knees. I buried my hands in his hair and ran my fingers through it again and again, now and then seeing if I could push him, steady him, direct his movements to satisfy my cock's imaginary pleasure. "Do you like it?" I asked him in a low, quiet voice, but he didn't answer.

I could feel the familiar pulsing of my cunt, and sensed that it was growing wet. I watched him suck me and tried to imagine my clit extending all the way up through the dildo and shivering under his tongue. I wanted him to take me deeper so I could feel his lips brush against my skin. I stroked his hair and looked down at him splayed against the sheets, and ground my clit up against the base of the harness. He sucked my cock even harder.

Soon both of us were ready for the next step. I pulled the dildo from his lips and nudged his shoulder, directing him to lie on his back. He complied, but wordlessly. I began to wonder how well I was doing, if he was bored with my soft touches, because he didn't moan or talk or cry out. I summoned my best indignant look and reached for the fly of his jeans, determined to make him respond.

He'd told me beforehand that he wouldn't be wearing underwear, and sure enough, when I unfastened the buttons of his fly, there was only his smooth skin and the base of his cock, pushed down against his thighs. I took hold of it and guided it out, feeling it swell in my hands.

It was lean and smooth and pale, just like the rest of him. It was also one of the longest cocks I'd encountered in my limited experience. It flopped this way and that as it straightened, somehow disconnected from the rest of his body, and his testicles seemed to stretch endlessly in the other direction. The cocks I'd been used to were shorter and made of stouter stuff; my hands were uncertain as they explored unfamiliar territory. The skin surrounding it was soft and hairless—had he waxed it just for me?

I slathered my blue cock with lube and directed him to lie on his back, feet up in the air. Like other, more staid couples, we would start with missionary. I straightened the tip of the dildo with my thumb, steadied myself, and began to lean into him.

He had to help me guide it inside him. I felt like a seventeen-year-old boy encountering a willing naked body for the first time, unsure of where to aim. But soon I could sense the slow glide of cock in asshole, and reached the place where the tightness of the opening gave way to sudden open space. His eyebrows rose while the rest of his face softened, and he hummed with pleasure.

"Be gentle for a minute," he told me, his eyes closed. So I ran my hands up and down his muscular legs, feeling their weight press against my shoulders, and pulled my hips back and then pushed forward again in a slow rhythm. I loved everything about his body, all leanness and smooth skin and muscles and curves, his strong jaw tilted upward. I found myself getting impatient with the slowness, wanting to push myself into him with all my strength.

"Are you ready to go harder?" I asked him, and he nodded yes.

I leaned forward and his legs yielded, bending closer to him. I drew my hips back, taking care not to let the dildo slip out, and then thrust back as hard as I could, holding his gaze. His lips were slightly parted and his eyes were full of longing, and I began fucking him in earnest.

In a low voice he asked me to kiss him, so I let his legs bend open and pushed the length of my body against his, my tits pressing into his chest. His kisses were hungry and open-jawed, and we mouthed each other ferociously, tongues darting back and forth, before I turned my head and pressed my lips to his neck and shoulders. He whimpered, just as I wanted him to.

"Are you my whore?" I asked him.

"I am," he replied.

I pulled out of him and he turned over, bending his knees and tilting his round and firm ass upward. He had the body of a ballet dancer. I dug my fingers into his flesh, gave him a smack with my palm, and began to guide the dildo in again, straightening it with my thumb. He had no more need for slowness; it was buried between his cheeks in a matter of moments, all the way up to the metal ring of the harness.

Fascinated, I watched my blue penis go in and out. His back was heaving; his limbs were splayed, froglike. What would it be like to feel with this thing, I wondered, to feel the inside of someone's flesh? I leaned forward and pushed my tits up against his back, raked my fingernails across his shoulders just to see the red marks. I was full to bursting with desire.

"You're mine," I told him.

"Yes," he breathed, barely audible. "I love you." The room fell into silence once again, only our disjointed breathing splitting the air.

The words gave me a start. I wasn't used to the word "love" coming up in dirty talk, except when specifically qualified: "I love your cock," "I love getting fucked...." It made me push myself closer to him, my breath on the back of his neck.

"Do you love me?" I asked him.

"Yes," he said. I made him repeat it.

I wanted to see his face again. I lay on my back, cock sticking upward, and he climbed on top of me and lowered himself onto it. I didn't want to stop thrusting, and found myself gripping his thighs and pushing my hips upward, straining against his weight. I arched my back and began moaning, feeling my legs rub against his skin.

His cock was in full view, falling to the side, and his face was creased with strain. I told him to let his head fall back all the way, and he leaned back to prop himself up with his arms. He wouldn't last much longer.

"Where do you want me to come?" he asked.

"On your chest," I said. I wanted to rub it all over him and see his skin shine with it. He gripped his cock and propped himself up with the other arm, stroking it up and down. His jaw fell open and his eyes squeezed shut as the semen spurted from the end of his cock, droplets landing on his chest and belly. I dipped my fingers in the puddles and raised them to his lips, and he immediately licked them clean.

"Don't stop just yet...let me enjoy it," he said, and he rocked back and forth, bearing down on me.

After a minute he climbed off the bed and cleaned himself off in the bathroom. I stayed on my back in the bed, the cock still strapped to me. After the fucking was over I knew it would look silly sticking up between my legs. But I didn't want to take it off, not just yet, while the bedsheets were still unmussed. I gripped it by the base and pushed it into my clit, feeling the blood course through me.

When he emerged from the bathroom he saw me still grinding against it. He smiled and took the cock in his hand, and at last I could see in his contented eyes the response I'd wanted from him. He began to rock the dildo back and forth in exactly the right place, and I gasped.

"*Now* you'll be able to feel it," he said.

SPRING FEVER

Giselle Renarde

Why Connor? I mean...Connor? Connor the Garrulous? Connor the Touchy-Feely? Connor the semi-closeted trans-curious sometime-cross-dresser? That Connor? Yes, that's the one.

Spring fever took the blame. The snow melted, the flowers popped out of the ground, the sun made its debut appearance after months and months of gray skies...and suddenly there was Connor. When did we start working together? October, it must have been. And in all that time I never gave him a second thought. I always liked him in a friendly sense. I knew I must because I don't usually let strange men touch me, even casually, on the shoulder, the back, the arm, as Connor always did. At first I kept thinking, *This is the sort of thing I would usually find creepy,* and yet it was impossible to see Connor as a sleazeball. He just wasn't that. He would touch the small of my back as he led me through a doorway and transfer the warmth from his hand to that curve of muscle and flesh. It was that feeling that makes you want to swoon, or dip like a ballroom dancer. It's that touch that makes a woman malleable as sheet metal—curvaceous sheet metal.

Thinking back, the first thing that impressed me about Connor was his basic ability to pronounce my name. I usually got "Dot-She" like my name rhymed with Hibachi. That's not right. It's "Doe" like "doe a deer, a female deer," then Che like Che Guevara. Connor just glanced at my name on paper—Dotschy—and pronounced it perfectly, even including the minor inflections lost on anyone who doesn't speak my language. Not that I speak my language. My parents' language, I should say. And here I'd been cursing them all these years for giving me such a ridiculous name. Now that Connor had spoken it, I couldn't be anybody but Dotschy. My name flowed from his lips like black velvet. Dotschy, dark and mysterious gypsy queen.

I can see why he thought I was a lesbian. Truthfully, I was making half-assed attempts in that direction for a while, flirting with this curvy girl, Ilina, who worked at the convention center. Connor must have noticed, which is a gratifying thought. Females seem to flirt with each other in this very meaningless way that makes it all the more difficult to break through the wall of friendship. Connor may also have taken me for a lesbian because, in our never-ending conversations on gender issues, I always had the lesbian feminist perspective to contribute. When I took sexuality and gender studies in university, it was the lesbian feminist approach or bust. You'd be struck down so fast if you even tiptoed around the cross-cultural model of gender relations—that's the whole "Men are from Mars..." fad. So Connor and I stood around lollygagging as he asked me these perplexing questions like, "How would you know you were a woman if you had no body?"

"I would know by my voice."

"No, because your voice is part of your body. See what I'm saying? If you had no body, how would you know you were a woman?"

What a baffling question. "I wouldn't, I guess. I would probably think I was a man, because I fit all the 'man' stereotypes better. I hate shopping, I never stop for directions, I'm competitive and combative, I'm obsessed with sex...."

"Well," he said, throwing his hands in the air.

"Or I might think I was something in between," I went on, not wanting to discuss my self-diagnosed nymphomania. "Or maybe, if I didn't have a body, it wouldn't matter. There would be no difference."

The day after that, Connor brought in pictures of a redhead with an air of distinction and a generous rack. "This is me dressed as a woman."

When the sun came out in April, I was instantaneously infatuated with the sweet transvestite. It was an all-of-a-sudden thing, a bolt-from-the-blue thing. Or maybe not. I analyze everything to death, I know, but I just had to figure out how I could go from affable to obsessive in under five seconds. What happened just before my abrupt transformation? He told me it was his birthday.

"No way. Seriously?"

"No, I'm just desperate for attention," he teased, shaking his head.

"That's so weird. It's my ex's birthday too. You have the same birthday as him. That's so weird."

"As him?"

"As him."

I guess that was the moment Connor realized I wasn't a lesbian. "Actually, I don't have the same birthday as him; your little boyfriend has the same birthday as me. I was born first."

"Oh, you think so, do ya?" I was getting ready to kick myself. Why was I heading down this road? I never told anyone but my closest friends... "And I didn't say 'boyfriend.' I don't do 'boyfriends.' "

"I thought you said boyfriend."

"I said 'ex.' "

"It's my birthday if I was born first."

"Well, aren't we the possessive type! You can't own a birthday." I was trying to shift the subject, but when Connor was on to a topic, he wouldn't let up.

"How old is your little boyfriend?"

Fine. "He's my ex and he's turning sixty today."

Connor was quiet for a moment, but expectant, like he hadn't heard me. "He's what?"

"Sixty. Six-zero."

I'd never witnessed Connor at a loss for words, but there was a noticeable gap between sixty and Dotschy. "All right, so I was born on his birthday, then."

"I'm a grave robber, I know." Why did I feel it necessary to justify my actions? And to Connor of all people!

He shrugged. "What? I'm not going to be judgmental about anything. People should be free to do as they please as long as they're prepared to accept the consequences of their actions."

I decided that wasn't a piece of fatherly advice. Looking at Connor just then, at his sparkling blue eyes, I was overwhelmed by a surge of adrenaline. I grabbed him by the lapels and squealed, "Oh, my god, Connor, you make me so excited!"

Where the hell did that come from?

Unlike most men, who are easily spooked by my predatory sexuality, Connor simply responded by opening his arms and saying, "Then give me a hug!"

He didn't need to ask twice. There was something physically magnetic about Connor. His body drew mine in. It was always like that. We never stood side by side, we huddled against each other like a pair of bunnies. When we spoke, we didn't maintain a respectable distance. We talked with our noses nearly touching, his head hovering over mine, me looking up at him, wide-eyed like the sorcerer's apprentice. That's how it always was. It didn't seem as though a hug could make much of a difference, but it did. He wrapped me in his arms. My mouth against his chest, I worried he'd end up with a lipstick stain on his shirt.

As he pressed my core against the softness of his paunch, concerns about dirty laundry melted away. His body felt warm and gentle, like a bubble bath. I could have curled up and lived in that hug. I don't remember what my hands were doing. They might have been petting his back, but I have no specific recollection. I have a bad habit of not reciprocating in these situations because I'm too busy absorbing the experience, absorbing the scent, which was almost floral on Connor, like a woman's deodorant. He was so soft. His body was like a woman's, but without the boobs. I melted against him, a waterfall of liquid chocolate.

When he broke away it was too soon, but we were at work after all. Setting off to our respective tasks, we chatted about the opera, then about some guy he knew who was in lunchmeat commercials. I forgot to check if there was lipstick on his shirt. It struck me as particularly strange, with the whole day to mull over my outburst and the action it generated, that I wasn't seeking meaning in it. Usually when I speak before I think, I end up wanting to bash my head against the wall. Maybe it was Connor's nonchalant reaction that made me so comfortable with this new knowledge that I was, without a doubt, infatuated with him. I won't say in love because with love, you expect it to be everlasting. I'd given up on the idea of love everlasting. With infatuation, you anticipate an end. And there always comes an end, no matter how promising it looks in the beginning. All is ephemeral.

Toward the close of the day I was desperately moving tables and chairs around, setting up for a charity dinner function. Connor came over on his way out the door. We chatted for a moment about work, and then he did something he'd done ten thousand times before, but that day it made me bubble: he said good-bye totally straight-faced, then he paused for a moment, then his eyes lit up and he smiled at me, and then his face went blank again. I don't know why, but that struck me to the core. I always spoke my mind, but it wasn't often I spoke my heart. "Oh, my god, Connor, you make me so happy. You have no idea."

Nearly wheezing, I breathed in recycled air. That was dangerously close to an "I love you," wasn't it? Connor smiled again. "If I make you happy, you should give me a hug."

I would gladly have given him more than a hug, but with so many people milling about…? "Yucky boy germs."

"I'm not buying that"—whole lesbian thing?—"after what you told me earlier." An arm around my shoulder, Connor pulled me into him and I was floating against the cushion of his belly. I dropped a handful of cutlery onto the round dinner table and wrapped myself around his center like a clingy child. This should never have to end. His hand was on the small of my back and it was warm, warm, warm, pressing me harder against his body. I wished he would kiss the top of my head. I waited to feel his lips on my hair.

"Dotschy, sweety, what's wrong?" There was another hand on my back. It was Hina's hand, Hina's voice.

Somewhat embarrassed, since this coworker of mine was

always making fun of Connor, I pulled away, but the man's arms kept me in place. Fine. I rested my head against his chest and looked Hina straight in the eye. "What's wrong with what?"

Hina looked from Connor to me, not much of a leap since our bodies were pressed together. Her mouth opened like she was going to speak, then it closed again. "I thought you were crying," she finally said.

"Nope."

"Oh." Hina stood staring at us for a moment, then set a centerpiece on the table.

"Hey Hina, let's do lunch," Connor offered, which was strange since it was late afternoon.

Hina rolled her eyes and scolded, "Dirty boy!" as she sauntered off, hips swaying.

I raised my head so my chin rested on Connor's chest. He looked down at me so our noses nearly touched. I hadn't brushed my teeth since morning, but strangely I didn't care. Connor's breath wasn't the freshest, but I didn't care about that either. Strange, strange, strange. The room was bustling around us, and we were the still point. "Do you think she's jealous?"

"Looks like," I said. "Do you think she's a dyke? I can't figure her out."

"If she hasn't fallen for you, she couldn't be. I'm sure even straight girls ask you out."

"No such luck. What was that lunch thing about?"

"I've been threatening to buy her lunch since before you worked here. She can't stand the idea. 'Ew, no way Connor!' "

It was almost a personal insult, that Hina would so forcefully reject a man I felt such a bond with. "Why, what's so gross about that?"

"It's not the lunch part, it's the dress part."

The dress part? Oh...I stood up on my tiptoes so my nose

met his. "You threatened to put on a dress and take her out on the town?"

Connor smiled. His eyes lit up. When he nodded his head, he took mine with him so our foreheads touched.

"You can dress like a woman and buy me lunch. We could make out in public and see if people throw stuff at us!"

"Uh...maybe we could hold hands..."

Shot down! Had I misread him? Then what was all this touching about? This insane amount of physical contact? Did the extent of Connor's affection stop at a hug? It seemed unlikely, and yet...I could easily have kissed him, with our faces so close, but I hesitated. He didn't want to make out with me. Damn.

"I do need the practice," Connor continued.

I smirked like a vixen. "Practice doing what?"

"Doing what? Going out dressed as a woman, what do you think? I've got more than enough experience eating a meal as a man."

"Oh, right." I thought he'd meant practice making out, but I wasn't going to tell him that now. I had no idea where we stood anymore. Despite the not knowing, I got caught up in Connor's whirlwind of planning activity. He was anxious to practice his feminine wiles in a social setting, and I was grateful to be swept into Connor's queer world. Man, woman...it was all the same to me. It was all Connor.

Connor, dressed as a woman, stood before me wearing a light pink sweater with those pearly plastic buttons down the front. It was the type of sweater a mommy picks out for her little girl. That's the spirit in which Connor dressed himself. Sure, he had plenty of life experience as a man, but he was a novice female. His skirt was a more mature tweedy gray shot with pink, slit in the back and just covering his knees. Did he shave his legs?

I couldn't tell, what with the panty hose. His shoes matched his sweater. His nails matched his sweater. They say redheads can't wear pink, but Connor pulled it off beautifully. He looked almost elegant, with his *Kiss of the Spider Woman* hairdo. His boobs were generous, but he had his natural paunch to match. Despite his height, he didn't look curiously tall. He looked perfect, actually. His glasses were the same pair he wore as a man. They suited him both ways.

Soft. That's the word for Connor dressed as a woman. He was soft. Soft pinks, soft body, soft curves. I ran my hand across his cheek. That was soft too. No trace of stubble. I'd wondered if I would be as attracted to Connor dressed as a woman as I was to Connor dressed as a man. "You look beautiful," I told him, kissing his smooth cheek, lingering close. Those sparkling blue eyes were Connor. The clothes were different, but the person was the same. I would easily have made out with him, and not just to see if we would get heckled by passersby.

"You look fabulous, dear," he replied, voice somewhat lilting, though neither high nor low.

"Fabulous? You're a woman, you're not gay. Try 'lovely' or 'gorgeous.'"

Into my ear, he whispered, "Dotschy, you're gorgeous."

My knees just about gave out. "Well, we had a deal," I responded, trying to stay casual, trying not to betray how fast my heart was pounding in my chest. "If you wore a skirt, I would wear one too." I'd worn a dress, in fact; tight and clinging jersey.

I still had no idea what I might get out of this date. Was it even a date? Was it two girlfriends going out for lunch? What was it? Connor had always been so transparent, but even in his transparency he was confusing me. He walked softly in his high heels while I stomped across the driveway in my platform sandals.

"So what's your name, Connor?" I asked as he unlocked my car door.

"Dotschy."

"Connor?"

"Dotschy?"

"What's your girl name?"

"Dotschy!"

"You can't have that name; it's mine!" I squealed, realizing the compliment.

"If your ex gets my birthday, I get your name," he shrugged, sauntering to the driver's side. He must have practiced a lot, because Connor walked better in heels than I ever could. I hopped into the passenger seat while Connor slide himself side-saddle into the car, tucking his skirt demurely beneath him as he swept his lean calves inside.

"Do you know how to drive in heels?" I asked. Connor looked with a certain amount of puzzlement down at his feet, which seemed to mean "no." "Because I'd really rather you didn't try learning with me in the passenger seat."

Eyes sparkling in the sunlight, Connor turned to me and, because of that whole magnetic body thing we had going on, I turned to him too. He leaned in and so did I, until we were sitting nose to nose in the front seat of his car. Connor didn't say a thing and neither did I. Why didn't he want me to kiss him? "Do you think you could seduce me dressed as a woman?" I asked Connor.

Rather than reply, he started up the car and pulled out of the drive like an expert in his pink heels. And there was I, doubting him. "Do we really have to share a name?"

"I like your name," he replied in that voice like a whisper. "Dotschy. It's pretty."

My heart leapt. "Thanks." Why couldn't I stop smiling?

We'd agreed on one of those Thai fusion restaurants uptown. Where else would you go with a cross-dresser? Since this was a social study for Connor, he was dismayed by the impersonal service we received. He really wanted to interact with people and see how a woman is treated in a man's world. But, hey, it was a busy restaurant. The servers had better things to do than play the pawns in his game. And for me, the whole idea was to spend time with Connor. As a man, a woman, whatever; I just wanted to be around him.

"Something's changed in you," he told me. "Just in the past few days. You don't blush anymore. You're flirty and cuddly and you never blush."

"I know what you mean, Con...Dotschy. Something's different now. Maybe it's because I told you about my ex, and that's not information I usually share with anyone. Maybe the sharing has bonded us somehow. You know, I can't stop smiling when I'm with you."

"I've felt a great affection for you," Connor began, "since we first talked about transgender issues. Usually when I bring up anything TG-related, people smile and nod and slowly back away. You were just like, 'Oh, yeah,' like it was a perfectly normal topic to discuss. That's uncommon. But I imagine you're so accepting because of your own past."

"My past?" I was puzzled. "Why, what have I done?"

"You dated a man, what, three times your age?"

"Twice my age, thank you very much. What, do you think I'm twelve? And, anyway, that's not so uncommon. What you don't see every day is a woman my age with a woman your age. We really should make out while you're dressed like this." My fingers slid across the table, toying with the gold links of Connor's watch. There were nicks on the topside of his wrist from shaving his arms. He must have done his legs as well, then.

It occurred to me, watching him sip and chew and pat a napkin against his lips, that "Dotschy's" mannerisms were not unlike Connor's. That's not to say that "Dotschy" was particularly masculine, but that Connor was a perfect balance of feminine and masculine in his everyday behavior. As I spun the loose gold around Connor's wrist, the server approached our table to offer the dessert menu. She looked at my fingers fondling Connor's nicked forearm for what seemed like a long time. "I'm stuffed," I replied. "How about you, lover?"

Connor's eyes went icy and wide. I raised my eyebrows. He pursed his pink lips. I smiled like a vixen. "Just the bill, I think," Connor said through gritted teeth and a forced smile. When she'd gone, he leaned in and, magnetically, I leaned in too. "One thing at a time. I need to be a woman before I can be a les—"

The server was back, looking for a place to slide the bill. We snapped back in our seats and she placed the black mint-stuffed bill jacket in the center of the table. "My treat," I offered.

"No, I invited you."

"Actually, I invited you," I insisted, but Connor had already retrieved his credit card from his purse.

"You're just dying to see how she'll react when she sees a man's name on a woman's card," I said, understanding what was going on.

Connor looked at me straight-faced, then flashed me his dazzling bright-eyed smile before his face went blank again. Connor...god, he made me happy.

The server took the card away, processed our bill and brought back the receipt, seeming not to notice the discrepancy between the male name on the card and the female person in the seat. I felt kind of sorry for Connor, like his experiment wasn't as useful as it could have been. When we walked through the first set of double doors leaving the restaurant, Connor wrapped an arm around my waist and before I knew what was happening, he was kissing me. His soft body—genuine paunch and false breasts—pinned me against the limestone wall as his warm tongue mingled with mine. He was taller than usual, wearing those heels, so I stood on my tiptoes as I wrapped myself around his neck. I'm sure some people walked by, but if they threw anything at us I didn't notice. This was everything I could ask for. He was Connor and he was soft, he was a man and he was feminine, he was kissing me tenderly and he was kissing me hard.

"Can we go back to your place, Dotschy?" I requested.

"Yes, Dotschy," he replied.

But we didn't get that far. Like a horny little rabbit, I pinned him against the car as he fished through his purse for keys. He looked down at me, eyes sparkling, and I looked up at him like Mickey in *The Sorcerer's Apprentice*. Our noses touched. The magnet pulled stronger. Our lips brushed. We kissed again. The idea of keeping my hands to myself while we drove all the way home wasn't working for me. We fell, still kissing, into the back-seat. Thank goodness for underground parking lots. Maybe no one would see Connor planting heavy kisses down my neck, peeling my dress straps down my shoulders and arms. His hands were large and soft. Pink fingernails, Connor! Pink! I took them between my teeth. I sucked his fingers while he exposed my tits, licking my nipples like ice cream. Everything was hard and soft. A hard lick, a soft kiss, a hard bite, a soft suck.

My head rolled back as he molded my breasts, tracing the dew my mouth left on his fingers against my rigid nipples. "This isn't why I invited you..." Connor began.

"It's why I came," I admitted, pulling a condom from my purse. "I hoped..."

Connor released a lever and the seat sloped into the trunk. So this was why people bought hatchbacks... "You want to...?"

His voice was neither deeply masculine nor liltingly feminine. It was just Connor.

"So badly..." I told him, turning his skirt until the zipper at the side faced the front. Pressing a bewildered Connor down into the slanted seat, I unzipped. He took off his glasses. "Oh, my god, Connor, you have the most beautiful eyes. You have no idea."

Under the silk hose, he wore these old-school panties like frilly boy shorts. Luckily the zipper on his tweed skirt was long enough that I could pull down his silky drawers and pull out his hard cock. It jerked forward in my hand. As I slipped on the condom, his pink-nailed fingers strayed under the cover of my thong. They slid slowly against my pussy lips until I lunged at Connor's mouth, sucking the breath from his lungs. "God, you're a good kisser, Connor."

He might have returned the compliment, had I let him up for air. I climbed on top of Connor dressed as a woman and eased him into my wet cunt. This was beyond my wildest fantasies, beyond anything I could have dreamed up. Kissing his mouth as I thrust my clit against his pelvis, I floated atop the pillowy paunch and big boobs concealed by a pink sweater. Grasping my ass, he massaged that yielding flesh in circular motions. I found the lever and pulled the seat upright, or nearly so. Wrapping my little bunny legs around his core, I moved on him slower and slower until I could feel every inch of his hard cock against every cell of my cunt. Arms around his neck, I lifted my body and descended, lifted and dropped.

We stopped kissing. He looked down at me and I stared up at him, our magnetic noses touching. His face was bright pink under the foundation and his eyes sparkled blue. I was breathing so hard my lungs seemed to take up half my body while Connor's cock took up the other half. "I haven't been this happy since...I don't know," I wheezed, unable to break away from his penetrating gaze. "You make me so, so, so happy, Connor."

The more I focused on my breath, the more rooted I became in the idea of Connor as the mighty oak in the sky that was me. He was yielding and powerful. I kissed him again, madly, pulling him into me, against me, everywhere at once. His hands were on my back, on my ass, squeezing, pressing, as his tongue fought wildly against mine. My whole body quaked as my cunt latched on to the stake driving through it. It was Connor. Everything was Connor. My core leapt and locked and I fastened myself to him like an insane koala bear as he whined and yelped and threw his head over my shoulder.

"Dotschy!"

"Connor..."

For a long while we sat like that, huddled together like a pair of sleepy bunnies. Breathing in unison into each other's ears, the greatest music was the panting, the sighing, speaking the lover's name again and again. Kissing my hair, Connor finally ventured forth into the realm of forbidden emotion. "Dotschy, I think I'm in love with you."

"Don't be silly, Connor. It's just spring fever."

THE MORNING TRADE

Angela Caperton

Josette Naveau unlocked the front door of Bean There, tying her fresh black half apron as the soft tinkling of door chimes announced her first customer.

"Josie? Darling, please tell me you still have that Tanzanian reserve you served last week."

Josie smiled when she saw Lianne Bester on the other side of the glass counter tucking her keys into the little Marc Jacobs purse that swung provocatively at her hip, an inch or two above the hem of her short, navy blue skirt. Lianne, amazing as always, Josie mused. Confident, self-possessed, and gorgeous, the tall, toned brunette with mile-long legs had never appeared mussed or rumpled in the two years Josie had known her, not even when the rumors about her brother-in-law Phillip had threatened the reputation of the entire family. More than the tailored suits and tight body, it was Lianne's aura that pulled people—especially men—into her orbit. Josie felt the gravity herself. She remembered the day Lianne had chased a reporter out of Bean There during the media frenzy over Phillip.

Eyes sparking with anger, Lianne had confided in Josie. "Josie, I love my brother-in-law. He's family after all, and while he's a world-class bastard sometimes and his tastes are even more exotic than mine, he's not a monster."

Even more exotic than mine?

The words had twisted in Josie for weeks after the conversation. The rumors about Phillip had been on every tongue, concerning his date with the daughter of a local banker that had gone badly off the tracks. She had not accused him of rape—she admitted being willing enough for sex—but the nature of the sex had frightened her enough to talk, and the sheriff and press had listened. That had been three months earlier, and Philip had kept a low profile in town ever since.

"Good morning, Lianne," Josie greeted her, with genuine affection. "Tanzanian reserve coming up." She looked to the door, then back at Lianne. "Do you want something to go for Mr. Bester?"

"Yes." Lianne's voice trailed off as she stepped behind the counter, her stiletto heels clicking sharply on the tile. Perfectly at home within the tiny shop's inner sanctum, Lianne bent over slightly, the skirt clinging to the curve of her bottom. Her blouse billowed away from her skin and Josie saw the delicate lace bra and the perfect swell of tanned breasts, the darker flesh of her nipples evident through the fine mesh. Josie's belly tightened as she smelled Lianne's skin, which gave off the faintest perfume of wet roses.

Josie imagined running her hand through the other woman's mink-lustrous hair. What would it feel like to touch another woman like that? What would Lianne do in response?

"Perfect!" Lianne said as she reached into the case and picked out a warm muffin. She straightened and her breast lightly brushed Josie's. Their eyes met and Josie looked away, feeling the blush in her cheeks. Lianne leaned forward and pressed cool lips to Josie's cheek, then pulled away, her brandy eyes gleaming with delight.

Muffin in hand, she clicked back around the counter and took her usual table. "Would you make Cass a tall of the Tanzanian to go? He and Pete have a breakfast meeting with the Chesapeake brokers so he won't have time to stay."

Josie's lips curved. "Pete's coming with him?"

Lianne's amusement turned her brown eyes to deep gold. "What's this? Do you like our appraiser?"

Josie's smile widened. "He's nice to look at and he's a good tipper. That's a good sign, right?"

Lianne laughed, low and sultry, then grew serious. "What happened with Mitch?"

Lianne put an insulator around the paper cup while the rich, exotic scent of coffee filled the shop. She didn't want to think about Mitch, and the disaster that had been their first—and last—experience in bed.

Josie stammered, her sense of failure in the presence of Lianne almost too much to bear. "He just didn't..."

Lianne raised one perfectly shaped eyebrow.

Josie shrugged. "Have you ever felt like you wanted more, you wanted something just out of reach, but you just couldn't see what that something was and you didn't even know what to ask for?"

Lianne's hand paused, a small bit of muffin held before mouth. "Yes," she said simply, nodding once before the muffin finished its trek to her crimson lips. She regarded Josie with shining eyes. "I have a philosophy, Josie. I believe each of us knows exactly what she wants. We just have to be honest with ourselves."

Josie's nervous fingers tapped the counter. "Maybe you're right, but then we have to be honest with other people too, right?"

"Silly girl. Everyone wears masks. Half the fun is removing them. You should let me show you sometime."

The meaning of that invitation hung in the coffee-rich air in the moment before the chimes rang again and the door swung open. Cassidy Bester strolled in, suit pants creased and his long-sleeved shirt starched crisp.

Lianne's husband—tall, lean, with broad shoulders and narrow hips—focused instantly on his wife. He crossed the room to her in three long steps. Josie often wondered if he and Lianne hadn't escaped from some fashion model farm, they fit together so perfectly. Cassidy's black hair, textured and tapered, crowned a face of strong angles with gray eyes that reminded Josie of brushed pewter. His generous mouth split into a wide grin before he folded himself over to kiss his wife.

"Hello, darling." His voice remained light, but the edges of it sparked with heat. His lips lingered on hers, their mouths working against each other. Josie turned to her coffee machine, but in the mirror behind it, she stared transfixed at the couple's reflection. Their mouths fused, Cassidy slid his hand into Lianne's blouse and cupped one breast, his thumb playing with the nipple. A trickle of sudden moisture slid down Josie's pussy. She turned back toward them as Cassidy slowly released his wife, his hand sliding out of the blouse as naturally as it might out of his own pocket. He planted a chaste kiss on Lianne's forehead before turning to Josie with a devilish smile.

Heat burned Josie's cheeks. Had she really just seen Cassidy feel up his wife? Different rules, she thought, different lives for people like the Besters. Erotic images frothed in her brain, the man across the counter playing the starring role in most of them.

"Good morning, my pretty barista," he said. "Is that the Tanzanian I smell?"

"She is pretty, isn't she, Cass?" Lianne asked. "There's something about her this morning that almost demands kissing, at the very least...."

They had played this game with her before, a flirtation that seemed innocent but quite sincere, not just sweet compliments to a girl in a shop, but something more. It still embarrassed her and she turned her attention to the coffee. She finished pouring it, put a lid on the to-go cup, and carried the drinks to the table.

Cassidy took a chair and relaxed as he leaned back, one arm draped over the back of Lianne's chair, his fingers tracing lazy patterns along her arm. Josie sat the coffee down and retreated. Why shouldn't they make love wherever they wanted?

"Where's Pete, Cassidy? Should I make him something to go?" Josie asked as she returned to her side of the counter.

"Only if you can deliver it to ten thousand feet. He's on a plane to Edinburgh. The Morrisons finally bought the Marie Alone," Cassidy told her, then sipped his coffee.

The chime rang again but Josie, caught up in the excitement of Lianne's delight, hardly heard it.

"One million?" Lianne asked as she picked at the soft inside of the muffin.

"One point two." The voice behind Josie was edged like a sharp knife, cold and hard.

Josie stiffened as she realized Philip Bester had come through the door. Cassidy's twin hardly glanced at her as he took a chair across from his brother.

Like a cloud on a pretty day, she thought as she wordlessly pulled an ebony, hand-tossed ceramic mug from the shelf and poured Phillip's coffee—always the same—dark French roast, black, strong, and served in his own coffee cup.

She brought the steaming cup to the table and set it in front of Phillip. "Can I get you anything else, Mr. Bester?" Josie asked automatically, the smile on her face as false as her pleasant voice. How could two brothers—identical twins at that—be so different? Seated across from Cassidy, Lianne between them, Phillip's appearance nearly mirrored Cassidy's—the same thick hair, the same gray eyes; their builds, even their walk was the same, but Josie could never mistake one for the other. Cassidy's full lips were almost always tweaked in a smile, a hint of mischief in his eyes, but Philip never smiled or, if he did it was only with grim sarcasm, and the gray of his eyes reminded her of the sea during a storm.

"Nothing," he said dismissively.

Josie returned to her place behind the counter while the three bantered about their business. She looked up when the chairs scraped and Cassidy and Phillip rose together. Cassidy came to the counter, winked at Josie, and put a twenty on the glass.

"Have a good day, sweetheart. Don't let the dockhands hassle you." Cassidy moved away, making room for Phillip who wordlessly put his exact change on the counter, the dollar bills pinned under the black mug, before he walked out of the shop behind his brother.

Lianne relaxed in the chair and continued to consume the muffin. "Oh, Josie! The remodel is finally finished on the house. You have to come over, especially after hearing me carry on for the last six months. Why don't you drop by tonight?"

Josie shrugged. She tried to imagine herself in their big Newport-style house out on the Point. She truly enjoyed Lianne and Cassidy's company, but what would she say to them? The Besters owned a world famous yacht brokerage. Maybe she could tell them about fighting with the milk frother in between their stories of Hong Kong and Paris.

Different worlds.

"I don't know, Lianne. I have so much to do after work." Could she sound any lamer?

Lianne popped the last bite of muffin in her mouth and washed it down. She pulled a silver tube of lipstick out of her purse and refreshed her lips.

"No pressure, Josie," she said as she twisted the stick back down. "But think about it. You're my friend and I'd love to share this with you."

Josie smiled and leaned against the display. "I'll think about it, Lianne."

"Call the office and get directions if you decide to come, okay?" She brought her cup and the muffin paper to the counter, and reached out to pat Josie's hand.

"Have a good day, darling," Lianne said, turning at the door to wink at Josie. "I'll see you tonight."

"Bester Yacht Brokerage," the gruff baritone growled on the other end of the line. Josie cringed. Just her luck—the evil twin, Phillip.

"Lianne, please?" she managed.

"She's not here. What do you want, Josie?"

"She told me to call for directions."

Phillip hissed. "Boca Road. Take a left at Madrid. Follow the road to the Point. The gate code's four-eight-two. Park at the second house. You'll have to walk from my house to Cass's on the boardwalk."

Before Lianne could ask a single question, the line went dead. She stared at her cell phone, scowling. "Prick," she muttered as she folded the phone and climbed into her car.

Blackness swallowed the road as Lianne drove beyond the gate toward the very tip of Reef Point. She saw the first house—Cassidy and Lianne's if she understood Phillip's instructions—

and understood why she had to follow the road to the second house. Scaffolds and heavy equipment still filled the sweeping driveway.

She drove past Lianne's house, where warm lights glowed in the downstairs windows, and approached the second, a smaller mansion, but worth more than Lianne would earn in her lifetime. Phillip's house lay shrouded in darkness save for lights bracketing its doors and a line of ornamental lanterns marking steps to a boardwalk that spanned low dunes and connected the two homes.

Josie parked and walked to the boardwalk. Surf roared beyond the path lights, salt flavored the air, and she wondered how it would feel to see the sun rise above the ocean every morning.

Night cloaked the boardwalk, the tall lamps spaced along its length dark, but starlight and the glow of Lianne's house guided and invited her. She strolled down the wood walk, and found the break in the wide railing that led to her friends' door, turned toward the house, and froze in her tracks.

She faced a bay window, clear as water, no curtains to obstruct the ocean view, or in the opposite direction, Lianne's bedroom.

Candlelight flickered from the corners and reflected on every surface in the room. In the center of the golden halo, a large four-poster bed stood, dark wood and black satin sheets shimmering in the glow.

And there on the sheets lay Lianne, entirely naked, with her bare husband kneeling between her parted legs, his body like a classical statue, chiseled and hard, his ass flexing in the dim light. Josie watched the muscles in his back bunch and ripple as he ran his hands over his wife's stomach and hips. Lianne arched, responding to every touch.

The ocean sang in harmony with the rush of blood in Josie's ears as Cassidy took a peaked nipple between his lips, his tongue playing at the stiff, dark flesh. Josie saw Lianne's lips part in a blissful moan and, to her shock, heard the faint sigh of it. Josie's blood froze. A sliding glass door to the right of the window stood open to the night air.

If she could hear Cassidy and Lianne, then they might hear her. What would happen then?

Mesmerized, Josie leaned against the lamppost and gripped the rail, her fingers curling over the edge of the windblown wood. She hardly breathed as her pussy slicked. Three more steps and she'd be off the boardwalk and on the path that led around the side of the house, or she could retreat, return to her little apartment, make a cup of tea, and rediscover the joys of masturbation.

In the room, as if Josie were seeing the action on a stage, Cassidy's hands worshipped his wife's flesh. He kissed her breasts, her neck, her lips. Lianne's body moved against his touch, her leg bending to caress his back and sides, her eyes closed, her lips wet and inviting. She pulled Cassidy to her, legs wrapping his waist, welcoming him, caging him.

He rose above his wife and looked down. Josie felt the intensity of his gaze and imagined how his eyes must look, gray flint striking sparks. He leaned over the bed and retrieved satin sashes the color of burgundy.

Lianne's laughter shivered down Josie's spine and wicked delight pooled in her stomach. Cassidy bit Lianne's shoulder, more than a nip, less than a rending. With all her soul, Josie wanted to be in that room.

Cassidy moved with easy determination. He turned his wife onto her stomach, pressed himself against her as he stretched her arms toward the headboard, and bound her wrists with the silken ties. An ornamental loop around the headboard secured her in tender but certain bondage.

He left her legs unbound. Lianne lay prone on her stomach

and Josie's mind spun with the delicious possibilities. Cassidy positioned himself behind his wife and lifted her hips from the bed. Josie saw his cock clearly for the first time, long and thick and very erect, before he forced Lianne's thighs apart and plunged it into her.

Lianne's thrilled screams echoed in Josie's center, louder than the waves, louder than her own racing heart.

Bare beauty pulled against the bonds, fingers curling around the ties, as Cassidy rode her with long, deep thrusts. Her breasts bounced with each impact, the rhythm of her gasps and groans of pleasure timed to each hard stroke. One of his hands slipped away from Lianne's hip, around the tantalizing curve of flesh, and between her legs. Josie saw the shadow of his pussy play, fingers working the folds and clit.

Josie's own hand slipped from the railing and slid inside the waistband of her light linen skirt. Her fingers edged under silky panties and through curls to tease her damp clit, as she watched Lianne fight the bonds and climb toward heaven.

Lianne's cries turned wild, her movements frenzied, when Cassidy thrust all the way into her and stayed there, half sitting, one hand under her stomach. With the slightest shift he reached down and from the tangle of sheets produced a crystal phallus. Smooth and ridged, the glass gathered flickering candlelight and became a shining golden cock.

He leaned over Lianne, his lips moving against her ear as she sagged against the bonds, her body quivering at the edge of oblivion.

"Do you want this?" Josie jumped at the words whispered in her ear. Her scream backed into her throat as a wet, salty hand covered her mouth. Struggling but held tight, she saw only a glimpse of a well-muscled arm and a wet bare hip. He smelled of the sea.

The weight of a dripping, muscled body pushed her against the railing, pinning her, soaking the back of her blouse, sealing it to her back. She attacked the hand that muffled her, nails digging deep, her fingers wet with blood, but he hardly reacted.

The voice—dangerous, dark, and concise, cut Josie to her heart. In the room, Josie saw Cassidy's lips moving and heard the echo—"Do you want this?"—warm and wicked.

Phillip.

What will she say?

Josie's pulse raced and her voice choked, stuttering for full release as cool lips, full and moist, traveled along her throat. She struggled against him, her mouth still silenced, his other hand invading her blouse, cupping her breast possessively.

"Shame on you, Josie, watching here in the dark," he whispered. "Whatever would they say?"

Shame and embarrassment stilled her, even as heat and power urged her to move. When he uncovered her lips, she made no sound, even as he jerked the blouse open, buttons no barrier against his purpose. He pulled it off her shoulders, keeping her arms pinned within the sleeves, then pulled it tight behind her. Wet skin pressed against her back. Chilled droplets of water fell from his hair, shocking her skin. His hand slipped over the exposed flesh of her belly, following the trail her hand had already blazed under the waistband of her skirt, his long, hard fingers invading the silk, until he found the wet bud of her clit and rolled it under his forefinger.

Rational thought fled as he slid his finger into her wet pussy.

He bit her earlobe. "Watch."

Panting, Josie obeyed and looked into the bedroom, where she saw Cassidy offer the crystal phallus to his wife's mouth. She lapped at it, her tongue eager, her eyes closed, lost in anticipation. With a slow grind of his hips, Cassidy pumped deep, and then he sat upright, still buried in her, and brought the glass wand to her ass.

With urgent force, Phillip pulled Josie's arms in front of her and bound her wrists around the lamppost. If she struggled, she could free herself, but his fingers found her pussy again and thought of flight evaporated. In an instant her skirt and panties fell to her feet. The sea breeze caressed her bare skin. She could scream, she could fight, but Josie knew for the first time what she wanted, and knew she'd do neither.

The thick bat of his cock pressed against her bottom, the crinkly hair around the base offering a tantalizing tickle.

His words echoed those of his brother within the candlelit bedroom. "Do you want this?"

Josie yielded. "Yes, oh, yes."

He folded her over the railing and swatted her hard on the ass. "Open up," he commanded her.

She obeyed, needing him inside her, bending to push her slit against the head of his cock. Inside, the crystal phallus teased Lianne's ass. Cassidy worked the glass into his wife's pucker with gentle insistence. Lianne began to buck in slow, rolling movements. Her cry was the wind and the waves and echoed Josie's as Phillip finally slid his hard, ridged shaft into her.

Josie bit her lip to keep a moan from shattering the night. The wet heat of his hips against her ass, and the unimaginable glory of his flesh pulsing inside her turned her bones to water. She sagged in her tattered bonds, the wood railing pinching the skin of her belly as her senses stretched with every long, splitting thrust.

She watched as crystal slipped in and out of Lianne's ass, the rhythm counter to Cassidy's cock action. His fingers still danced with Lianne's clit, and she began a keening that Josie wanted to echo.

Sea-cool flesh slapped against her ass, faster, dizzying, the pleasure building to frenzy as Phillip fucked her, tangled and trapped as she was. He circled and massaged her clit until Josie's vision blurred. Through the gauze of pleasure, she watched Lianne rock and pant, her beautiful face a sweaty mask of bliss. Higher Josie soared, the cock pounding into her driving her, pushing her, slick satin-steel transforming her soul, as wave upon wave of divine sensation plunged deeper.

Deeper to find...

Her teeth pierced her lip, blood pooling in her mouth as the peak loomed, her clit tight, her pussy constricting as orgasm stretched her senses to bursting.

Deeper.

Lianne screamed as Cassidy slapped her asscheek hard, his handprint red in the golden room. He thrust mercilessly into her, rocking the bed, the glass phallus all but disappearing in Lianne's hole, as the couple came together, Cassidy's beautiful back and buttocks rigid with his release.

Deeper, delving, diving, finding.

Pearls.

Josie found her strength as the orgasm peaked. She pulled against the shirt, her muscles constricting at once as crashing pleasure stole her breath, splayed her open, devoured her like a morsel served on a gold plate. He gripped her hips, his rhythm faltering, but his thick cock still fueling the waves of pleasure. One hand freed, she found his on her hip, covered it with her own, and pulled him deeper as she pushed back, clenching his cock with her pussy. Nails found purchase and raked as the orgasm drowned her.

She barely heard his growl, but the heat of him pressing against her back and the warm wetness slipping down her legs needed no voice. Unbearably tender, he kissed her shoulder, then closed his teeth into the muscle and claimed her entirely with one last thrust of his semihard cock.

He unhooked her makeshift bonds and she melted into his possession, eyes closed, her ragged breath barely filling her lungs.

She wanted the moment to freeze forever, but the sea never stopped its assault on the sand, the wind insisted on stirring her hair, and the sweat that covered her body began to dry.

He pulled out casually and turned her to face him, but the darkness hid his expression. He lifted her chin and kissed her, his tongue teasing, licking the blood from her lip, promising. Then he pulled away and turned her so her back and ass molded to his front, his cock pulsing with new life.

In the open door, Cassidy behind her, Lianne watched, naked and glowing, her hair tousled, her hands stroking his encircling arms. She stared directly at Josie, the smallest smile upon her lips, but before Josie could voice anything, Phillip turned her again and obliterated her senses and any traces of guilt or shame in a searing kiss. Waves crashed upon the shore, the stars slid across the sky, and in a haze, Josie gave herself to her own desires.

The chimes on the door rang. She shut her eyes and braced for the moment she'd been dreading.

"Darling, let's be adventurous." Lianne's honeyed voice called from the other side of the counter, "We'll both have a cup of the Kenyan roast."

Josie tightened her mouth into a forced smile. Lianne wore a perfectly tailored short black dress and Cassidy a blue suit without a tie, his shirt open a little. They smiled at her without a trace of smugness or even recognition of what had happened the night before, settled at their table, and divided a newspaper.

Josie watched them breathlessly until Lianne looked up from

the financial section. "Are you all right?" she asked.

Josie jumped as if struck by a whip. "Kenyan! Yes, coming up."

The chimes sounded again and Phillip came in. Her heart tried to beat out of her chest as she approached the table with the coffee. Phillip, his short-sleeved polo shirt accenting his well-muscled torso, sat on one side of Lianne and Cassidy on either. Phillip smiled coolly.

They all watched her silently. Her cheeks burned and her hands trembled as she started putting the cups on the table. She stared back at their mouths, remembering the kisses shared and witnessed, the bites, the hands, the heat and wind. She went wet with the memory and smelled her own arousal.

Distracted, she set Cassidy's cup on the edge of the table. Quickly, he reached for it before it fell to the floor. Across the back of his broad hand, Josie saw three furrows, angry and fresh, and Josie's heart climbed into her throat.

"Something wrong, my sweet little barista?" he asked with the smallest smile.

She shook her head as she met his gaze. Not Phillip. Phillip had been with Lianne.

Different rules. Different worlds.

Lianne grinned at her, her red lips wet and inviting.

"Do you know what you want now, Josie?" Lianne asked her, one hand on Phillip's thigh, the other on Cassidy's arm.

Suddenly unbound, Josie felt as though she might do anything, as though she might fly.

"Yes," Josie answered, surprised at the firmness in her voice. She met Lianne's gaze, then Cassidy's, and finally Phillip's. Both men's eyes promised storms.

"Yes I, do," Josie breathed. "I know exactly what I want now."

THE RAT-CATCHER

Layla Briar

The plumber calls "Ma'am," and I come around the corner. He has a fistful of what looks, at first, like wet straw. On closer examination I see that it's a tangle of condoms. I blush; then frown, because this will never do. He's so beautiful, with his compact muscles and fresh haircut, but there's no way I can seduce a man who handles other people's waste with his bare hands. It demonstrates a cavalier attitude toward hygiene. I sigh; another one down.

I explain the condoms by telling him that my nephew was here dog-sitting, in February, while I went on a cruise. This is perfectly true. I have used condoms, myself, the last few times I've had sex, but I know enough not to flush them. And it's been a while, anyway. Since October, and Carlisle.

The plumber jokes with me, pleasantly; he asks if maybe my dog-sitting nephew could give him some pointers, maybe teach him some fresh pick-up lines. "There must've been a dozen rubbers down there."

"Well, Ryan's a hottie."

"Zat so?"

He washes his hands, and I make a mental note of everything he touches—faucet, soap pump, towel—so I'll know what to disinfect later. It's such a shame; he has lovely hands, with straight fingers and smooth, square-trimmed nails.

"Boys or girls?" He pushes a button on his remote control, and the plumbing snake retreats backward down my hallway, leaving a glistening trail.

"What?"

We back up together toward the kitchen, him wiping the floorboards as he goes. "Does your nephew like boys, or girls?"

"Are you gay?"

He straightens, nodding.

I snort with laughter, and keep on laughing. The plumber smiles, confused. I love this guy. He's warm. He's the opposite of Carlisle. When I finally regain my composure, I offer him coffee. He accepts.

"Ryan is straight." I offer the plumber the sugar bowl, noting where he touches it. "I'm sorry for laughing at you. It's a long story."

He leans against my sink to indicate he's got the time. He's wearing gay-guy clothes, I realize now. A T-shirt with a supple drape, an Italian brand of jeans. As gay as you can get away with in rural Ontario. Boy, am I ever thick.

"It would offend you," I tell him.

"Naw."

I know it won't, anyway.

I tell him I belong to a book club, all women, all around my age. "I'm fifty-two," I add. He nods.

"Well, we generally read literary fiction, you know, serious stuff by serious authors. But for a change, a few months ago, we read this trashy chick-lit thing; they're always about slutty junior editors, or PR reps—anyway, it was so cliché that the protagonist actually seduced the pool-cleaning boy in one scene."

"As if a slutty junior editor could afford a pool."

I smile. I love him. "Well, exactly. And then we women got to talking amongst ourselves, and the big debate was, how possible is that, really? To seduce a tradesperson who comes to your house?"

I'm half-hoping he'll answer my rhetorical question; I wouldn't mind his perspective. But he stays silent, keeps smiling, so I go on. "About half the women said, piece of cake. Any woman can seduce any man, anytime. The other half said, no way, José."

"And you said?"

"I said I wish I'd taken the trouble to find out, back when I was young and sexy."

He laughs. "You're still sexy, hon."

I smile at him, gratefully. "Well, I hope so...because they dared me to, and I accepted."

"You bet them you could seduce a repairman?"

I nodded. "They gave me a year to make good on the bet. This is an old farm. Things are always breaking down. And there's no husband to fix them." I raise my eyebrows provocatively.

"And I was a prospect, until I told you I'm gay?"

I shake my head. "Until I saw you with that handful of used condoms. Eww."

He frowns in mock offense, and I press an extra twenty into his hands with the credit card slip. On his way out, he spots Ryan's graduation photo on top of my piano, and taps it with a finger. "What a shame. Bet I could convert him."

"Out!" I shoo him playfully through the door and watch him pick his way gingerly down the frozen walk.

* * *

Before the gorgeous gay plumber, there was the furnace guy, a middle-aged fellow named Rocco who showed me pictures of his six children, four girls and a boy. Way too married.

Then two months later, the furnace conked out again and they sent someone else, an earnest man with an accent, balding but young, maybe in his late twenties. I flirted my heart out with *that* guy. He answered mostly in monosyllables, until he got on a rant about the son he'd fathered back home in Albania when he was eighteen. The mother was a monster, an evil jezebel bent on denying the boy a life of comfort here, in Lambton County.

I told him I felt his pain. I told him everybody needs a little comfort in this life. I told him we deny ourselves the company of others, and for what?

I sucked lasciviously on a candy cane. I considered putting vodka in his tea. But it was no use. Miz Boland this and Miz Boland that, through two days of clunking around in my freezing cellar. When he passed me in the doorway, he'd suck his stomach in and flatten himself against the jamb lest any part of his body touch any part of mine. It was useless.

And so, when I'm fed up with whatever it is that's shredding the insulation in the eaves of my garage and call the rat-catcher, it barely registers that the man they send is unpromising—a stern farmer-type, perhaps seventy years old. I lead him to where I keep the ladder, and I go in to make coffee.

Five minutes later, there's a howl—then a thud—in my side yard; and the unmistakable odor of skunk percolates through the cracks in the siding. I hurry to the window, and the rat-catcher is on his knees, digging blindly through his bag. He pulls out a white plastic bottle, wrenches off the cap, and splashes the contents into his face with both hands. I hold my breath and struggle with the old window, stiff even in this dry cold. It's been shut since fall.

There's a blast of cold air and then the skunk tang hits, making my eyes water even at this distance. Before I have a chance to ask what I can do for him, the rat-catcher is barking orders.

"Hose! Towel—an old one." He's facing me, but he can't see; his eyes are scrunched tight against the assault. His white hair stands on end all around his face, giving him the look of a mad professor. "Is your outside water on?"

I run to the shutoff to check, then to the shed for the hose. When I get back, he's wearing only a pair of graying, stretched-out briefs. I hesitate. "You know, you could come inside and shower. It can't be more than six or seven degrees—"

He grabs the hose from my hands. "You don't want me inside, ma'am. House'll stink for months."

I believe it. Just being near him, I know that the smell has permeated me, too—my hair, my pores. I back away.

"Did you not expect to be sprayed?"

He snorts. "Didn't expect a skunk. Not in rafters. Skunks don't climb."

"Oh, no?"

"Towel," he growls, turning the water on.

The rat-catcher turns, dripping, at the sound of my next approach, and I can see that his stomach is preposterously flat, his midsection almost concave above the abdominal muscles. But the skin on those abs is old-man skin—thin, and losing its grip on the structures beneath. I find myself staring; I don't hand him the towel immediately, even though his shriveled nipples are blue with cold. Instead, and without ceremony, I reach out and place my free hand on that flat belly.

We look down together and watch, with a detached interest, as the slight bulge in his sodden briefs lengthens, then rises, straining against the wet cotton.

When the rat-catcher meets my gaze, he doesn't smile; instead he frowns and appraises, gauging my intent. This strikes me as funny and I want to ask him, sarcastically, if this is a common occurrence, for strange women to test his virility. But I can't even open my mouth. He is dour and frowning and I am frozen to the spot. He is also spectacularly hard, for an old buzzard—well, how would I know, not having fucked anyone his age?—but the head of his cock has actually fought its way out of a leg hole and is inches from my elbow. I look in his eyes for permission to touch it; I feel suddenly much more like a naughty child than a seductress. But his expression doesn't soften. He takes the towel from me and steps backward for room to dry off.

With his long fingers, he rakes the elastic of his briefs down over his hip bones, and lets them drop to the ground. He stands front-on to me, cock at full salute as he dries his hair, and there's an unmistakable threat in this. His leanness makes him nakeder than naked. He's grandpa-old and teenage-hard and he's smack in the middle of my side yard in March. The bare branches of my mock-orange bush rattle icily against the drainpipe and if anyone drove by right now, they'd surely crash into my mailbox at the sight of him. I look down at his bony white feet on the frozen grass and the lewdness of just that little detail makes my breathing shallow.

He walks toward me and hangs the towel on the railing. The skunk smell is so strong that I teeter when he leans closer, the wind behind him now. He kisses me roughly, his gums bony under his thin lips, hard teeth just below the surface. He scoops up handfuls of my long skirt in each fist—trying to get at me right there next to the tap—and I have to squeak, "Indoors," as if he didn't know any better, like an animal not quite tame.

Even then, I lead him only as far as the antique church pew in my entrance before he sits, stubbornly, and yanks me toward him. When I stoop to pull my panties off, my face comes within inches of his cock but I'm thinking instead of the hose, in summertime, and being a child in need of a drink. I imagine the mineral-and-rubber-tinged reward, excess water dribbling on my shoes, the rest icy at the back of my throat. And so I open my mouth, but he won't allow that; he impales me on him instead, and I fumble for a handhold and find none. I'm forced to flatten my palms against the wall for traction.

His thighs are hard and shockingly cold. His cock is cold. I have never felt such a thing before. My face is so close to the wall that I have to turn my head sideways, and my cheekbone bumps hard against the paint, twice, three times, and he's done. It's only then, too late, that I even begin to feel aroused myself, or, at least, become aware of it. I linger in his lap until his eyes open, and he eases himself free of me with a shudder.

The rat-catcher offers no apology for the brevity of his performance. We're both farming people; I guess he assumes I'm familiar with the concept of buyer beware. Buy a truckload of someone else's compost, and you've accepted the risk of crabgrass; seduce an old bachelor who hasn't done it in this decade and bear the risk of premature ejaculation.

He's looking around now, realizing there are no clothes at his feet to pull on. His overalls and jacket are outside, in a heap at the top of my driveway. He clears his throat and steps around me, heading for the door.

I frown. "You're not going to put those back on? They're only good for burning. You'll never get the smell out. I'm sure I've got something that'll fit...."

And then, halfway up the stairs, I get angry. Not at this man, specifically, or even at Carlisle, who's been the reliable target of my wrath for five months now. Not even at men in general, just for being nothing like the pool boy in that stupid novel. Perhaps I'm angry at myself, I reason, for being so willing to scurry in search of clothes for this ungrateful old grouch? But that's not it either.

By the time I've reached the top of the stairs, I find I've completely changed my tack. Instead of digging for a sweat suit, I get purposefully under the covers of my bed, and I call down to him. "Are you coming?"

He's quiet, and I imagine him standing with his ear cocked, wanting me to repeat myself, but I won't. I wait. He waits. A long moment passes and I savor his confusion. I finally hear his footsteps creaking on the old stairs, and a broad smile creases my face.

The rat-catcher appears in the doorway. My bed is going to smell like skunk forever, and I wish I'd thought to use the spare room instead. But what's done is done. He shifts uncertainly on the rug until I actually hold the covers up and pat the mattress for him to sit. He lowers himself onto the sheet and, as angry as I still am, I suddenly feel a strange tenderness toward his frail body: the extreme boniness of his hip, the blue rings that span his nails at the cuticle. He's going to need half an hour at least, I reckon, to get it up again; but that's fine, and it serves my purpose. I take his hand before he's even properly settled and I lay it on my hip. When he doesn't move it, I put my hand over his and move it for him, gliding his smooth, dry palm along the skin of my inner thigh.

I put him to work. I press my lips to his but wait to be kissed, keeping the pressure on until he reacts. I part my knees emphatically and hold his gaze.

And so, the rat-catcher reaches grudgingly for me. He parts the lips of my pussy and slides his fingers into the cleft. He does this dutifully, almost absently, in his farmer's way. I know his kind. The situation confuses him, but duty is familiar.

After a moment or two I'm surprised at my body's eager

response. It takes effort to hold my own hands back. The coolness of his lean body tempts me; the thinness of his skin is strangely intimate, promising access to all manner of textures beneath. Even the skunk smell doesn't repel me; there's a purity in the way it overwhelms, leaving room for nothing else.

But I restrain myself and I make him work.

When I'm close to coming I fight that too. I retreat at the last moment and kneel facing him; I stare impassively and wait for him to follow me to his own knees, to cup my breasts in his hands. My skin is thinning too; my nipples droop a few inches lower than they used to but I find I want his practical, farmer's eyes squarely on me. I want to be seen just as I am. I want to be assessed, appraised—maybe even found wanting; and to be pleasured anyway.

He's obeyed this far, and so I give up some ground: I let my hands drift where they may. My fingers find the slight swell of his bottom, the only place on his body that's even remotely fleshy, and it's my touch, once again, that arouses him. The rat-catcher is used to work; manual labor is all he knows. He's used to handling bodies, even if they're the bodies of animals. It's gentleness, and mercy, and being touched that are exotic to him. With my hands on his body, his mouth is instantly softer and hungrier, and I don't have to look down to know he's hard now. I reward him by pushing him onto his back, and I climb astride and ease him slowly inside me. We look down at our genitals and not each other's faces while I accomplish this; our lack of emotional connection has left us free, and we find ourselves fascinated, like children.

I ease my way into a rhythm, careful of my own comfort. I take my time. I glance down as I grind against him, and it pleases me to find that the rat-catcher's eyes are closed. He is not searching for my gaze; he doesn't demand engagement; he does nothing to compete with the rhythmic grip and slide of woman on man.

There's a dignity in this quiet self-possession. What made me angry earlier—what I perceived as an inappropriate attitude of entitlement—moves me now. I lean forward, instinctively finding the angle that will bring me off and as I do this I put my hands in his wild hair and we come, exactly together, my fingers wrapped gently around his thin skull.

Afterward I'm careful what I talk about. I don't want to ask him what he does for a living besides pest control, in case, say, he raises minks for fur. Or in case his politics offend me. So we stick to pleasantries. I serve him coffee. I don't offer to pay his fee, because he never did oust my vermin, and so he would feel patronized. I don't tell him he was the best lay of my life. I lend him sweatpants and an old flannel shirt.

As he drives away, I know what he's thinking, because I know his kind: that it's not true what they say. Some skunks *do* climb.

HIGH HEELS

Elizabeth Colvin

I know it's about the high heels. I know that, but I don't care. Because the feet in them are mine, and feeling you worship them is the same as having you worship me.

We go out for dinner at a nice restaurant. I wear a sexy dress, but not too sexy, because it's not the important thing. Neither are the pearl earrings, the makeup, or the way I wear my hair. What really drives you crazy are the heels, four-inch stilettos in red patent leather. I wear them without stockings, leaving my painted toenails exposed and my ankles circled by just the slimmest of shimmering straps.

You try to take your eyes off of them, but I won't let you. We get a table in the corner so I can reach out with my foot and delicately tease your leg. You glance down at them and I can see the effect the high heels have on you. Your face reddens and you keep glancing down at them.

When no one's looking, I slide one heel up the inside of your leg and nudge your cock. From the way you squirm, I can tell it's already hard.

After dinner, we go walking in the park, and I take care to walk delicately, nudging my hip against yours to draw attention to the clicking of my heels on the sidewalk. Your breath is coming short. Your eyes go from my feet to my face and back again. They always rest longer on the feet.

We find a secluded bench, somewhere no one on the street can see us. There are other couples walking, enjoying the warm, romantic night. City people walk their dogs, barely giving us a second glance.

If I told you to, you would drop down on your knees and worship my feet right here. But instead, I curl myself onto the far side of the bench, one foot under me, and put my other foot in your lap. Your cock surges against my foot as you begin to caress me. Your fingers trace the contours of the shoe gently, finding the places where the strap touches my bare skin. I've always had sensitive feet, and I shiver with every caress. Luckily it's a warm night.

Every few minutes, I casually nudge my foot into your crotch, as if to reassure myself that you're still hard. You are, and every gentle touch I give you makes you want me more. I can see it in your eyes. I can see it in the way you look from my feet to my face to my feet, trying hard not to let your hips grind against me too much. When people pass by us, I ease my foot out of your crotch and let it rest on your thigh as you stroke it. Just a poor working woman, I appear, tired from a long day, getting a foot massage from her devoted boyfriend.

By the time I take you home, you're mad with desire. I tell you to make me a drink—it's asking, really, but both of us know that tonight you wouldn't dream of denying me anything—and I strip off my dress, sitting casually on the couch. I prop my feet up on the coffee table and look at you hungrily as you approach with my wine.

You don't even have to say it. You hand me the wine, drop to your knees, and push the coffee table out of the way.

My feet are so sensitive that it tickles as your tongue embraces my toes. But every stroke of your tongue sends a surge of energy directly to my cunt, and as you get more and more excited, you tongue me more enthusiastically. With the dress gone, I'm wearing only panties and a bra. Normally I would have worn a garter belt and stockings for a dressed-up night like this, but I wanted my feet naked under the high heels. You lick your way up to my calves, worshipping first one leg, then the other. Your tongue caresses the ankle straps, then licks down across my feet and savors the place where the leather cups my toes. You lick your way to the underside and begin to caress the soles.

As you lick the soles of my shoes, I set my wine on the side table and my hand descends into my panties. I'm wet—gushing. My cunt throbs as I begin to rub my clit. I slip two fingers inside me and press against my G-spot. I return to my clit and rub in little circles as my excitement mounts. You move on to my other foot and hungrily devour that stiletto, too, taking a moment to lick up to my fleshy heel, pampered by today's pedicure. The feel of your tongue on my bare flesh brings a shiver to my body. I rub my clit faster. Then I lift my foot, and you know what I want.

As you take the stiletto heel into your mouth, swallowing it as if it were a cock, I whimper. I want more.

"Take your cock out," I tell you.

"Yes, Ma'am," you answer, your mouth coming off of my stiletto heel for only the time it takes to say it. You unzip your pants, take your cock out, and begin to stroke it. I can tell from the way you're breathing that you're very close. But you won't come until I tell you to.

I rub my clit faster, harder, feeling my orgasm approach. You hold my ankle delicately in your hand as I wriggle back and forth on the couch, my hips grinding involuntarily in time with your strokes as if I were fucking your face. Your mouth glides back and forth on the patent leather, your lips glistening with spittle. I cry out as I come, and in the middle of my breathy moans I tell you to do it.

"Come," I order. "Come on my feet."

Your mouth slides off of my shoe and you lean close to me, your cock pointed directly at my feet. I push them together so you can baptize them both at the same time. I see the effort on your face, your cheeks flushed with excitement. You let out a groan and your cock explodes, shooting come on my feet. The hot stream sends a pulse of energy through me, and you pump your cock until you've bathed my feet in your come.

You lick me clean as I sip my wine, smiling.

"Tomorrow we'll go shopping," I tell you. "I saw the most adorable set of pumps downtown."

"Yes, Ma'am," you tell me, and hungrily kiss my heel.

THE WOMAN IN HIS ROOM

Saskia Walker

Luke had a woman in his room.

I could hear the familiar sound of his voice—gravelly and seductive—as it filtered out of the partly open bedroom door. I paused on the landing and listened. There was music playing in the background, something sensual and rhythmic. Then I heard the woman's laughter, and something inside me altered.

The small part of me that was still immature balked because it was some other woman, and not me. But the part of me that was a young woman who was becoming more deeply aware of her own sexuality—the part that had been stimulated by my exposure to Luke in our home—responded altogether differently.

Desire, and the sure knowledge of my own needs, flamed inside me. The crush I had been nurturing for Luke changed. It wasn't an ethereal emotion cloaked in sighs of longing and wistful glances anymore. It was hard-core lust. And I liked it.

I liked this feeling of being a woman who had physical needs that were more powerful than her daydreams. I could just as easily be that woman in Luke's room. I wanted to be that woman, it was as simple as that.

I'd wanted Luke since the day he moved in, three weeks earlier. I doubt my father would have let his business partner stay over after his wife threw him out, had he known that I would develop an obsession with him. Dad thought I was far too busy at college. Too busy to notice a man like Luke? No way.

"You've met Luke, haven't you, Karen?" my dad had said when Luke walked into our house that first night, a suit carrier flung casually over one shoulder, an overnight bag in the other hand. I remember being glued to the spot, thinking that I'd surely have remembered him if I'd met him before. Apparently I had, briefly. Four years earlier. I guess I'd been different then. I'd been fifteen and a tomboy. Now I was at college, and my focus was on the adult world, with all its risks and discoveries.

Luke had set down the bag he held and put his hand out to me. "You've grown up," he said under his breath and looked at me with an appraising stare that made me feel hot all over.

I managed to put my hand in his. He held it tightly, drawing me closer in against him. I looked up into his wickedly suggestive eyes, and it made my pussy clench.

My mother disapproved of him. *Why did his wife throw him out?* she demanded of my dad, when Luke was out of the house. Dad wouldn't answer. I made up my own reasons, fantasies that featured me in a starring role. Maybe he left his wife for a hot younger woman, me. The truth was that Luke moving in had made something shift in my world. He was a man, a real man. Sex with him wouldn't be like the fumbling bad sex I'd had with a guy I met at college. As soon as I saw Luke, I knew that it wouldn't feel like that, not with him. Sex would be exciting, maybe even kinky. The idea of it fascinated me.

Luke wasn't what you'd call handsome, but he was attractive in a bad boy sort of a way. Tall and leanly muscled, his body suggested athletic vigor. His features were craggy, his hair cut close to his head. He had a maverick quality about him that appealed to the dark side of my imagination. At night I'd lie in my bed and imagine there was no wall between our rooms and that I could reach out and touch his body. I'd imagine him responding. He'd climb over me and screw me into the bed, teaching me what it was like to be fucked by a real man.

During the day when he was out I would go into his room and touch his things. Sometimes I even lay down on his bed. I would close my eyes and breath him in, getting high on the smell of his body and his expensive cologne, the experience building up a frenzy of longing inside me. What if he walked in and found me there? The idea of being caught by him made it even worse. Sometimes I'd push my hand inside my jeans and press my panties into the seam of my pussy, massaging my clit for relief.

Then my parents went away for a fortnight, leaving me in Luke's care. Oh, the irony. If only they had known how much the idea of it excited me.

It was our first night alone, and I had been thinking about him all evening, barely aware of the blockbuster movie I'd gone to see with my friends. I wanted to get home, to see if Luke was there.

But now he had a woman in there with him, and that woman wasn't me.

I was intensely curious, and it struck me that I was getting hot just thinking about him having sex, even if it wasn't me he was having it with. The push-pull reaction of the unexpected situation had me on edge. Torn, I glanced at my bedroom door. He probably thought I was in there, asleep. Like a good girl. I looked back at his doorway and saw a shadow move across the room beyond.

His shadow.

I couldn't walk away.

Luckily I hadn't switched the landing light on. I was glad of the darkness, glad that I was standing in the gloom and that his door was open and I could see into his room. I'd had a couple of beers earlier. That probably helped, too. I stepped farther along the landing, until I could see him.

He had his shirt off. I'd seen him seminaked before, in the kitchen in the mornings. He'd have a towel round his waist, his body still damp and gleaming from the shower. I managed to muster up an early morning conversation so I could watch him pouring out coffee, stirring in three teaspoons of sugar as he chatted to me easily, watching me all the while. Watching me in a way that made my body feel womanly and alive. That's what he'd done to me; he'd made me feel alive. And although I remember saying something in response to his early morning conversations, it wasn't what I was thinking. What I was thinking was X-rated. I wanted him to bend me over the breakfast bar and introduce me to real sex.

The woman was sitting back on his bed, and he had his knees pressed against hers. As I watched, he bent over her and pushed her silky red dress up along her thigh, exposing her panties. Craning my neck, I could see that they were very small, a narrow strip of sheer black fabric. Luke stroked the front of them, and when he did her hips moved on the bed, rocking and lifting under his touch.

My pussy ached to be stroked that way. My pulse was racing. Would he strip? Would I see him naked, as I longed to do?

He spoke to her in a low voice. I couldn't hear what he said. Then he straightened up and she also moved, into an upright sitting position. The light was obscured and before I knew what was happening the door opened wide and Luke's shape filled the frame, a dark silhouette against the light behind him.

My hand went to my throat, but there was no time to try to escape.

"Well, hello," he said. He didn't sound surprised. Did he know I'd been there, watching?

"I was at the cinema, just got back." I could hear my own breathlessness. The light was behind him, but I could see that his fly was open, the belt on his jeans dangling suggestively down his thigh.

"I knew you were out here, Karen," he said more quietly. "I heard you come in. I was waiting for you to get back."

I stared at him in stunned silence. He knew I was here. He knew…he knew I wanted to go into his room and be with him, that was what he was insinuating. I could hear it in his tone. Did he know I'd already been in there, on his bed? I could feel my face growing hot.

He pushed the door wide open. The woman was sitting on the bed looking in my direction with a curious expression. Perhaps it mirrored my own. Even from here I could see she was pretty. She had jet black hair and a smile hovered around her ruby painted lips.

"Come in, join the party," Luke said. The casual remark was powerfully suggestive. It went right through me, thrilling every ounce of me. He lifted his hand. He was holding a glass, and I heard ice chink as he shifted it from side to side invitingly. "You know you want to."

I did want to. That's the moment I addressed what was inside me, what I was becoming—a woman who could be proactive about her desires. I had a choice, but I knew what I wanted, and he'd invited me closer to it. I stepped past him and into the room, my entire skin racing.

Tension beaded up my spine when I heard him close the door.

He stood at my back. I had to force myself to breathe, telling myself over and over to chill.

The woman sitting on the bed ran her fingers through her hair as she looked me over, her body moving in time with the music. "You're even prettier than Luke said you were."

She knew about me? That was when it hit home. He had planned this; he'd told her about me. Should I be annoyed? I looked at her more closely. She was maybe a couple of years older than me but she had an edge, a self-assured confidence I knew I didn't have, but wanted.

She patted the bed beside her, and when I sat down, she lifted a tumbler from the floor and offered it to me.

Luke followed and stood close by, at the foot of the bed. When I glanced his way, I got an eyeful of bare chest and open fly. Just what I wanted. The only part I wasn't sure about was the other woman.

"I'm Lisa," she said. "I'm glad you came to play with us...."

She was flirting with me.

I didn't think it was possible for my temperature to rise any more than it already had, but it did. *Okay.* We were going to "play," and I didn't think she was referring to a card game. She was looking at me as if she were deciding which item of my clothing to take off first. Luke, half undressed already, smiled down at us. I was getting the gist of the setup now. He wanted two women. As long as one of them was me, I figured I could roll with it.

But the way she was looking at me...that did weird things to me. She was very sexy. I found I wanted her to flirt with me some more. I swigged heavily from the glass. It was whiskey. The potent liquid washed over my tongue and, when I swallowed, the hit was just what I needed. "Thanks," I said as I handed the glass back, and tried to look as relaxed as she did. Crossing my legs, I rested one hand on the surface of the bed.

Luke smiled down at me, approvingly. I had to take a deep breath to stop myself from grinning like an idiot. Jesus, this was really happening. All I could think was: *Thank god for the whiskey.*

The woman, Lisa, sprawled easily onto the bed beside me. When she got settled she reached over and ran her hand down the length of my hair. I stared at her, and when she paused with her fingers close against my neck, I smiled. She moved lower, touching my breasts briefly through my T-shirt, before wrapping her arm around my waist and drawing me closer to her.

I rolled onto the bed next to her and she kissed me full on the mouth. I was stunned, and stiffened. I'd never kissed another woman before then. But then I melted, because she was all soft and yet full on, at the same time. I felt the urge to answer her, and I kissed her back.

Oh, how delicious that was. For a moment I almost forgot that Luke was there. Almost. When I looked back, he had a gleam in his eyes and the bulge at his groin was larger. Between my thighs I was aching with longing and with him looming over the pair of us I felt the urge to be wild, to explore. I pushed my hand into Lisa's silky hair, and drew her in for another sweet kiss.

"Oh, yeah, you're delicious," she said, approvingly as we drew apart, pushing me over onto my back. She laughed gleefully, and it was infectious.

I bit my lip, but couldn't contain a giggle.

"You're really horny, aren't you?" She pulled my T-shirt up over my breasts and off, as she asked the question, then squeezed my nipples through my bra.

"I don't suppose there's any point in denying it," I responded, another laugh escaping my mouth when she shoved my bra to one side to tug on my nipple.

Before I knew what was happening, she had my sandals off, and my jeans undone. She wrenched them down my hips. Playfully, she lifted my panties and put her hand underneath them, touching my pussy. She watched my face for my reactions. My breath was captured in my chest. I glanced at Luke, who was looming close by. He looked as if he was about to pounce. I couldn't predict what was going to happen next, and that thrilled me.

When I didn't resist her, Lisa pulled the panties off of me as well. Luke looked me up and down. I lifted my arm and drew it over my face, closing my eyes, unable to watch him staring down at me when Lisa moved between my thighs.

I'm doing this with a woman, and Luke is watching. I felt slightly crazy, lack of control and sheer horniness sending me dizzy with pleasure. And then I felt her mouth close over my clit, and every nerve ending in my body roared approval.

Her tongue moved with purpose, tracing a pattern up and down over my clit, driving me mad. Her hands were locked around the top of my legs, her thumbs stroking the sensitive skin on the inside of my thighs in time with the movements of her clever tongue. This was alien to me, to have a woman service me, but it felt so fucking good and I didn't want her to stop. My head rolled from side to side on the bed, and I cried out loud, unable to keep it inside. "Oh, oh, fuck, it's so good."

She knew just what to do, and when I was thoroughly wound up, she nudged at my clit with the tip of her tongue until I came, my body writhing as I spasmed and fluid ran down between my buttocks.

She rose up to her knees on the bed, and then she pulled her dress off in one long slow move. She was naked beneath, aside from that tiny G-string that barely covered her shaved pussy. She was sleek and lissome. Her breasts were small and pert, nipples hard and dark. Tossing her hair back, she looked down at me. "Fuck her now, Luke. She's so ready."

My face burned up, but she was right, boy, was she right. I shot a glance at him to see his reaction to her comment. He nodded at me when he saw me looking his way, and when he did, I clenched inside, my gaze automatically dropping to his groin. He undid the final two buttons on his fly. His cock jutted out from his hips, hard and ready. Holding it in an easy grip, he reached into his pocket with his free hand and pulled out a condom packet.

My hands were shaking, I knew they were, and I pressed them down onto the bed to keep them steady. I couldn't stop myself. He really did mean to use the condom on me. I stared at him rolling the rubber onto the hard shaft of his cock.

Lisa had moved to one side and was watching expectantly.

I could scarcely believe it. The surprise must have been there on my face, because Lisa chuckled softly and reached in to kiss me again, easing me back down the bed. When I was flat against it, her hands roved over my breasts, and then she captured one nipple between finger and thumb, tweaking it. As I glanced down, I saw that her other hand was in between her thighs, where she was stroking herself.

"I like to watch, it makes me hot," she whispered. She flashed her eyes at me, and then her mouth closed over my other nipple, her teeth grazing it.

Tension ratcheted through me. My eyes closed, my legs falling open, and then I felt the weight of him, right there between my thighs, his hard erection pushing against me.

"Ready for me?" he asked, when my eyes flashed open and I looked at him. He was lifting my buttocks in his hands, maneuvering me into position, his cock already easing inside.

I managed to nod. I was so slick from Lisa's attention that he acclaimed me in one easy thrust, the head of his cock wedging up against my cervix. I moaned aloud and my body closed around him, gripping his hardness in relief. Pleasure rolled through me when he drew back and then thrust again.

Lisa was sucking hard on my breast and the pleasure arced through me to my core, where Luke was riding me hard, massaging the very quick of me with his cock. My orgasm was coming fast. I panted, hard. I reached out, gripped on to his arm when wave after wave of pleasure hit me.

"Oh, yes," he said, and thrust deep, staying there, while his cock jerked, sending an aftershock of pleasure through my sensitive cervix that made me cry out.

It took a full minute for me to catch my breath.

Lisa was snuggled up against my side, and she kissed my shoulder affectionately when Luke went the bathroom.

"What about you?" I said, without thinking, brushing her hair out of her eyes.

"I'll get mine." She smiled. "Don't you worry about that." She winked at me.

"How you doing?" Luke asked as he rejoined us, lying on the opposite side of me to Lisa. He cupped my buttock with one hand as he asked the question, and smiled that wicked smile of his.

A breathless laugh escaped me. He knew just how well I was doing.

"Good, I'm doing good." I returned his smile, and then glanced over my shoulder at Lisa to include her. She made me curious. That hadn't gone away.

"I meant to tell you," Luke added, "I'll be moving out when your parents get back."

My hands tightened on his shoulder, and my smile faded. I didn't want hear that.

He squeezed my buttock tighter. "You'll have to come round and visit me in my new apartment."

I nodded, quickly.

"Both of you," he added.

At my back, Lisa chuckled softly. I felt her breath on my shoulder. Soft, seductive, and warm. She moved to spoon me, her hand stroking my side affectionately. I had her—so alluringly feminine—on one side of me, and Luke on the other—hard, hot, demanding, and all man. Something joyous and liberated in me reveled in the decadence of it, the blatant mutual pleasure.

"I'm up for it," Lisa said, as she clambered over me, pushing Luke down on the bed and straddling his hips. "What about now. Ready for more?"

"Too right." He reached for the bedside table and grabbed a box of condoms. When he did, she winked at me again.

Could I watch him with her? A small residual doubt ticked inside me, but I couldn't look away when she grabbed a condom packet off him, opened it, and rolled it onto the stiff shaft of his cock. Mounting him, she put her hands on her hips, circling on the head of his cock. The crown pressed into her slit, and I watched, mesmerized, as it eased up inside her, splitting her pussy open before my eyes.

The sight was so hot that my hand went to my clit, and I thrummed it as I watched her riding him. A moment later Luke reached out to me, pulled me closer, and kissed me, thrusting his tongue into my mouth. The doubts inside of me slipped away. I was being introduced to a world of sensuality and erotic possibility.

And I was ready, ready for all of it.

WITH A SMILE ON YOUR FACE

Jana Corell

You're waiting for me with a smile on your face, candles lighting the bedroom. You know you're going to get some, I've made that much painfully clear to you. You know I'm hungry for you. You know that when I said, "You've got to do *exactly* what I tell you to," I was not just looking for a night of bossing you around; I was planning on using you more soundly than I would ever let you use me, and we'd find out if your claim that "We could still have some goddamned good sex," holds water.

The breakup was mutual, but you wanted to retain benefits. That I withheld them but never gave you a solid no kept you coming around, flirting, reaching, biding. And if you've learned anything, it's that biding your time with me usually works; I'm always too hot for you to turn you down indefinitely. The last six times have just been strictly about stubbornness on my part, and the fact that you didn't stop didn't annoy me the way it should have. In fact, it made me finally tell you not so much what I *want,* but what *you're about to give me.*

Or rather, I didn't tell you. But I'm about to.

Knowing you're about to get laid always puts a fucking smug smile on your face. That's why I'm about to put that smile somewhere I won't have to see it.

You're stretched out on the bed, looking as good as ever in jeans and a tank top and bare feet. I told you not to dress up; this isn't a date. You're wearing clean white briefs under the jeans, which are low-slung enough that I can see the underwear. The jeans are tight and I can see a small bulge; I know you well enough to know you're about two-thirds hard, not quite three-quarters.

As I enter the bedroom you see I'm wearing a skirt and high heels and a low-cut blouse, and I can tell it has an effect on you. I can tell it makes you turned on and cocky and smug—as if it were possible to be any smugger than you already are.

Your body fluid and strong, you get up off the bed and say, "Hi," and come toward me and move to embrace me. I want to melt into your arms and let you fuck me silly, but there's no way I'm going to let that happen. Instead, I meet your advance with a flat palm against your perfectly muscled chest, the very touch of which makes me go weak. But I manage to stay strong.

I shake my head and say firmly, "No."

"I thought—" you begin, but I shake my head again and put my hand, fingers slightly spread, across your lips.

"Exactly what I tell you to," I say.

You shrug. "Okay," you say, cocky verging on annoyed. A dozen post-breakup come-ons, and you're only getting annoyed now. The cruel part of me hopes that lasts, but most of me just doesn't fucking care.

"Whatever you want, baby," you say, equal parts peevishly obedient boyfriend and passive-aggressive sensitive New Age guy. "Just tell me what you want."

I grab your face, my thumb flat against your jugular, feeling your pulse quicken. I look into your deep chocolate eyes and fight back the urge to collapse.

But I don't. Instead: "I want," I say, "your fucking clothes in a pile on the floor." I take a hard breath, twist my lips in a sneer. "All of them. And you on your fucking knees."

There's this long pregnant pause where I'm not sure if it's working; I've practiced it a hundred times in the mirror, and each time sounded only slightly less ridiculous than the last. I can't let myself break eye contact, because I know if I do I'll be letting go of your jugular, in more ways than one.

Your pulse thrums faster. I hold your eyes hard, ice in my breathing. You don't drop your eyes for what feels like minutes, but it's got to only be a few seconds. I'm afraid for a moment that you're going to grab my wrists and flip me onto the bed and fuck me without another word, without even taking my skirt off. And maybe that would work, too.

But you don't. You drop your eyes, finally, meekly, and I steal a glance down your front. You're not two-thirds hard any more, not even three-quarters. You're more like hard-and-a-half, your breathing fast and your pulse going jackhammer quick. Your hands are shaking as you reach for the tight bottom of your tank top.

"And don't call me *baby*," I growl.

Your hands paused and bunching white cotton under your pectorals, under your hard nipples, revealing your perfect belly—you always work out more when you're "between relationships," which I guess this counts as—your eyes meet mine again, so wide and deep and rich I could fall right into them.

"What do you want me to call you, then?" you ask, your voice defiant.

"I'm open to suggestions," I say firmly, my hand still at your throat.

You think about it, lift your tank top over your head. I withdraw my hand as you do. You reach for your belt as I saunter over to the bed and kick off my high heeled shoes.

"Ma'am?" you ask me earnestly, working your pants open.

I shrug. I sit down on the pillow, leaning up against your big headboard, which I've gripped so many times while you fucked me. My thighs are pressed together and my bare feet tucked to one side.

"Lady?" The jeans make it down your thighs, revealing your briefs, bulging big and firm and clean and white. There's a wet spot where your cockhead has swollen against the cotton, almost to the waistband.

I purse my lips and cock my head and then shake it vigorously.

You peel down your briefs and your cock pops free. I spread my legs and the skirt climbs almost to my waist. I'm not wearing anything underneath.

"Mistress," you say, the word catching in your throat so it comes out as a thin squeak.

I look at you disdainfully. "Excuse me?" I ask.

"Mistress," you repeat.

I smile. "That works," I said. "But you're not going to be calling me much of anything for the next hour, *baby*, maybe more. Your mouth's going to be busy."

I spread my legs wider and turn toward the edge of the bed.

You're there in an instant, leaning forward, trying to kiss me. I catch your unkempt mop top in my hand and push you down, leaving your big full lips quivering in denial. You go down nice and easy onto your knees, and I guide your mouth between my legs. It's open, and you're making a whimpering noise; I can't tell if you're trying to say my new title, or if you just can't stop the moan escaping from you.

It doesn't fucking matter, because what I want out of your perfect mouth can be given without vocal cords. And as I wrap my thighs around your face, you give it to me—your lips, your tongue, making my own mouth pop open and a gasp explode from my throat.

You go to work with fervor, showing the same skill that made me see stars on our very first date. Oh, my fucking god, the things you can do with that tongue. Your lips made me hungry for you the first time I laid eyes on you—big and bee-stung and feeling so fucking incredibly good nestled against my cunt, just the way I knew they would. But it's your tongue that really makes me crazy; it's something about the way it's so wet and supple as it goes to work on my clit. It makes my eyes cross and my ears ring, and I haven't had nearly enough of it since the first glorious time you did this.

I remember so clearly how it happened: You were after me, I was reluctant, I wasn't ready, whatever. Then there was our all-night "talk" in this very bed, fully clothed, "talk" meaning deep conversation interspersed with making out, fingering, and most of a hand job. When the sun threatened to burst through the windows and it seemed pretty clear I was not going to fuck you, you got my panties off and did this, just like this, your mouth like magic—seduction and aggression and sheer pleasure, pouring into me like you loved my cunt more than anything else in the world. An hour later I was wrapped around you, taking you deep inside, and desperately calling your name.

But that was a year ago—too long. I was too easy; fucking was always an option, and I never made you work for it. I didn't want to demand; I didn't want to ask. You got what you wanted, always, and this glorious gifted mouth only dipped between my legs for the swift licks of foreplay, never for seduction.

Now, though, you're staying down there. An hour, I told you, an hour, maybe more. I don't have to rush. I don't have to worry about getting wet so you can fuck me—I'm already as fucking wet as can be. I don't have to worry about coming; I can take my time and let you get me there slowly, the way you know how to do.

And you *do* know, like no guy I've ever been with, like no guy who's ever bothered to spend an hour with his face between my legs—which is to say, no one. You know exactly how to tease my clit, work your tongue tip across the hood and down underneath so I gasp, and then down around my lips and shallowly into me, your lips pressed against mine. You know how to use your hands, too, but you're still cocky, down there, maybe thinking you're going to get laid. You reach up to unbutton my blouse, and I catch your wrists and say, "Uh-uh," and point your hands toward my pussy. That's when you say it: "Yes, Mistress," and I go all gooey inside, even before I feel your thumb and forefinger parting my lips wide so you can slide two fingers easily into me.

There's something about your cock that doesn't quite hit my G-spot; it's your fingers that do it, every time, and I'm gibbering. I can feel it swelling against your fingertips deep inside me, as your tongue works my clit and your lips caress mine intermittently. I relax into the bed; I stretch out on it. I clutch your pillow and smell you mingled with the scent of burning candles; when you look up at me, I meet your eyes and tell you, "Keep going," breathlessly, because I know I could come any minute but I want to savor it. "Don't fucking stop until I tell you to, *baby*."

"Yes, Mistress," you repeat, and launch into your task with newfound hunger. It's like you've been waiting your whole life to devour me, and now you've got your chance. I mount closer and closer to orgasm and keep fighting it off because I don't want to give in to your perfect tongue—not until I've used you well and thoroughly. I have one moment of doubt where I prop myself up on my arms so I can look down and see it—your cock, erect and pulsing between your legs, showing me you wanted this as much as I did, if not more.

That's when I finally relax into a bed that smells like you in a room that smells like candles, and I let you finish me off. You know I'm almost there, and you play me like a virtuoso. It's a tiny, girlish noise that comes out of me when I come, my pelvis working rapidly and my hand pushing hard on your head. I climax so hard I almost don't notice the sound I make, but I just barely catch it—and I know it makes you smug.

Which is why when I'm finished, when my body's warm and glowing, I sit up, grab your hair in one hand and your throat in the other, and bend you back until your perfect ass tips over your ankles and you hang there tottering.

I look into your face, see the glistening juices of my sex, and bend down to kiss you, but don't. Instead, I lick your face, feeling it hot with excitement and tasting tangy with my cunt.

Then I look into your eyes, see the surrender in them, the way I wanted. I look down and see your cock.

"Come on," I said. "You can go ahead."

I don't have to clarify, and I don't have to tell you twice. Your hand wraps around your cock. You groan softly, a strangled sound behind the oh-so-light pressure of my hand beneath your jaw. It takes five strokes, or possibly ten. I see your eyes roll back and feel the hot sensation of your come on my upper arm.

I let go of your throat, press the wet streak on my arm to your mouth. I'm almost surprised that you open for it, and lick me clean—obediently.

"What do you say?" I ask you.

"Thank you, Mistress," you say, your voice thick as if your well-worked tongue is swollen.

I leave you there, kneeling, wet with my come and yours. I stand, pull down my skirt, and stretch in the candlelight you've lit to seduce me. Truth be told, you did a pretty good job.

You're still kneeling there wet, slick and dripping as I pause at the door and look back at you.

"You know," I tell you. "I think you're right. I think we really can still have some goddamned good sex. Can't we?"

I don't wait to find out if you say it behind me; if so, the door's already slammed before you do. But that doesn't matter, *baby*; I already know the answer.

TWO STRINGS TO LEON'S BOW

Anais Morten

Flirting lazily with Leon again, I wonder when he will make the first move to go any further. Not that I'm afraid of taking the initiative if necessary. In fact, there's something rather attractive about men who know how to enjoy passivity. But I'm always curious to learn how a man expresses himself when it comes to hitting on a woman. It reveals so much of a man's personality. And especially with Leon it will be very interesting. Trust Leon to not rely on any common standard pick-up formulas!

But god, the man really isn't in a particular hurry, and my libido rapidly loses its limited patience. There is no progress, in spite of all the promising looks with those infamous, wonderful blue eyes, and in spite of the shocks of electricity he shoots through my system whenever he's randomly touching me—and he does that deliberately, I swear! He's like that, a human stingray, able to apply a deadly dose of venom with one finger. He stirs up my blood in a sly and completely unfair way with his sexy voice when we're rehearsing our scenes together—mind you, he literally fills my ears with the fluid, raw, pure essence of masculinity...Oh, I lost my train of thought....What I wanted to say was: though he winds me up and turns me on and thrills me through and through, the bastard hasn't taken this anywhere near what I need. And I need it soon.

Now there he is, chilling on his seat in the pub, right across the table, idly leaning back and watching me through frayed lashes, an annoying smile in the corner of his wicked mouth. Damn him. His dark hair is shoulder length, framing his angular face with those high cheekbones. His hands...no, I won't go there. Damn him, damn him again.

Suddenly he turns his head just a little bit, his eyes slowly wandering sideways...and I can almost see his look flitting off like a laser beam, crossing the room—and when I follow his look, realization hits and almost knocks me off my seat.

It's Alan over there, leaning at the bar, apparently relaxed, but I can see the tension in his muscles. He receives Leon's glance like a gift, catching it and acknowledging it with a nearly imperceptible graceful and grateful look.

One look, and suddenly it's all so obvious. How could I fail to notice it earlier? Leon has indulged Alan with tender attention that is far too constant and refined to be nothing more than an ironic game to embarrass the blond man. Okay, the rugby tackles and other sorts of affectionate rough handling one can pass off as some more of his crazy jokes, but in retrospect I can recall more than enough moments during filming when Leon's hand lingered just a few seconds too long on Alan's back; when he stood just a little too close; when he eyed him in a way that was simply too...how can I describe it? Too desirous, too admiring, too challenging, too lascivious, too threatening—all at once.

In a flash of a moment I remember one event especially: Alan had brought a bottle of wine to one of our informal cast meetings, and Leon ran into him—intentionally, as I know now but didn't know then—and Alan dropped the bottle. There was a thick carpet on the floor, so it didn't break when it fell. Alan immediately got down on his knees to pick it up. Leon roughly grabbed his hair and held him down. Alan froze; my breath hitched. Leon gave a hoarse, throaty laugh, like a wild Indian in a cowboy movie who's just about to scalp his victim. But instead, Leon slid gracefully down on his knees beside Alan. With sudden kindness and warmth in his eyes he placed a little kiss on his cheek, robbed him of the bottle, and jumped up again. Elastically springing into the middle of the room he uncorked the bottle and announced the party started. Alan still knelt on the floor, confused.

How on earth could I have ignored the obvious right in front of my eyes? But hey, it was Leon, and everybody knows that he's stark raving mad. How clever that craziness is...you can hide your intentions so well behind craziness!

Leon, that bastard, had been flirting with Alan all along, but I was so busy going after him myself I overlooked it. Usually I'm not that blind, so that concerns me a bit, but now is not the time to contemplate the implications.

My eyes meet Alan's and I have the strange impression of looking in a mental mirror, because Alan grasps for the first time what's been going on between Leon and me, too. We stare at each other in mutual bafflement and momentary hostility, and Leon looks back and forth between us with increasing amusement. Bastard! We look back at Leon, then at each other, all in all creating a fascinating spiderweb of looks across the room.

I wonder what will happen next, who will come out swinging first. I bet it's Alan, judging from the shivers of rage that are shaking him now; he will hardly be able to maintain his posture much longer. He fires looks of open jealousy at me. He will throw a fit and make a scene, that's for sure.

But—this seems to be the night of unexpected turns.

Silvio appears out of nowhere and flings himself onto Leon's lap. At once he starts whispering excitedly in Leon's ear, and Leon uses the clueless boy as a shield, only glancing over his shoulder once to assure himself that Alan will not fall into action as long as Silvio is present. So now Leon's hiding behind a living barricade. Coward!

Barely a minute later Silvio drags Leon out behind him, still talking miles a minute. Not that Leon truly wants to resist. Actually, he's more than relieved that coincidence provides him with a pretext to leave the soon-to-be battlefield; we both can see it in his gloating eyes. He shrugs back at us both in an excusatory way when they pass the door, but his sarcastic smile betrays him.

Alan and I exchange another look, and I sense the honest pain in his gaze. There is only one way to get back at Leon now.... I walk over to Alan. His expression quickly changes to firmly closed while I approach him, but there's a spark of new interest in his beautiful sulky eyes when I let myself fall against the bar with my back next to him and simply murmur, "Slut," pointing vaguely in the direction where they have disappeared with my chin.

"Who?" growls Alan. I can tell he's still undecided between turning his back on me and cutting me off, which certainly is his first impulse, or taking up the conversation which would enable him to maybe get some detailed information about what I have in mind with Leon and how far I already have proceeded—pretty much the same things that I want to get out of him.

"I meant Leon," I specify. "Because it goes without saying for Silvio."

Alan chuckles, and I'm pleased to see that he is not jealous of Silvio, though he is jealous of me. In fact, I feel a little honored....

To me, it's totally clear that Leon wouldn't sleep with Silvio. If he did, my interest in Leon would die immediately. But Silvio is young and Leon is crazy, so there's a natural intersection of their interests. Silvio probably talks him into jumping between rooftops or crossing the road on their hands or whatever.

"Do you think he will decide which one of us he wants to fuck anytime soon?" I ask out of the blue, without any further preamble.

As intended, I catch Alan by surprise. He bites his lower lip and blushes to the tips of his ears, instantly lowering his lashes and his head, trying to evade my searching, scrutinizing gaze.

"Don't tell me he already fu...you already slept with him?" I almost shout, incredulously. Alan flinches at the volume of my voice, and if he could blush any more and lower his lashes any farther, he most certainly would. He cringes.

He will not be able to bring himself to answer within the next half hour, that's for sure, so it's no use torturing him any more. Slowly, it dawns on me that Leon has simply kept me on the reserves bench.

"I'm sorry, Alan...I didn't know...or else I wouldn't have...I won't flirt with Leon anymore. Forgive me."

I'm about to retreat and bow out politely, but suddenly Alan grabs my arm and pulls me back.

"No."

"What?" Yes, this definitely is a night of unexpected events.

"I don't want you to give him up and sacrifice your own purposes for my sake. But most of all, I want him to make that decision, not you. I don't want to be beholden to you for your generosity." He hisses it sharply, and that alone is so sexy that it wouldn't need the gratuitous effect of his intense eyes boring into me.

"Okay..." I drawl, very flustered and intimidated, and Alan slowly releases my arm from his painful grip. "So...how about we share a beer?" I chirp meekly, and he grimly nods.

I have never had a real conversation with Alan before, but it doesn't take long before we've got our heads together, whispering with heated cheeks and shining eyes. Maybe it's due to a few too many beers, but also because it's good to talk to him and he seems to like me, too. I can tell the whole experience with Leon is hard to take for him, and he badly needs someone to spill his heart to. And though you usually don't trust your adversary, as his rival I also have a lot in common with him. Leon has made fools of us both.

I learn that Alan has had sex with other men before, but it has been a while and it has never felt like it does with Leon. They had the most stonking sex together—I swallow enviously when Alan murmurs in my ear that Leon sometimes fucks him twice without ever moving out in between times...he simply stays in Alan while he rests heavily upon him, until Alan feels him growing hard inside him a second time...and Leon starts thrusting again. Believe me, it didn't help my riled-up nerves to listen to Alan's raspy voice whispering these kind of confessions in my astonished ears.

But though the sex was all he ever dreamed of, Alan still doesn't know what it means for Leon. Leon never explains himself and Alan never dares to nail him on it, and Leon is a terrible tease, always playing around and flirting around with everyone.

Later that evening we have a meeting. The director gives the schedule for the next few days; there are always changes because of the weather and other actual circumstances. When Alan and I arrive, Leon's already there, and after exchanging a conspiratorial smile, we sneak up behind him and sit down on both sides of him.

Leon quickly looks to the left, then to the right, and he stiffens a bit, but also grins surreptitiously. I can tell he feels somewhat uncomfortable, but thinks he's clearly in charge. We just stare straight forward to where the director is preparing for his explanations, and Leon also doesn't talk to either of us. Only after the room is crowded with members of cast and crew do Alan and I start to flirt with each other literally behind Leon's back. We not only lean a little back to look each other in the eyes, we also lay our arms on Leon's backrest side by side, and stroke each other.

Leon is shifting in his seat—he knows what's going on directly behind him, but doesn't want to show it affects him. He's ticking like a time bomb. Alan and I both know it and grin at each other gleefully over Leon's broad shoulder. How come you can see the expression on the face of someone you know very well, even when you only see him from behind? I don't know how, but Alan and I knew exactly when Leon's eyes narrowed and his lips shrank to a thin line.

He's getting really nervous, and suddenly he gets up and leaves with his long fast steps, never looking back, though the director stops in the middle of his sentence in surprise and then calls after Leon. Leon only walks faster, and after calling him twice more the director shrugs and carries on. Leon does crazy things, after all.

As soon as he's gone, Alan shifts closer, taking Leon's seat. Seeing his gorgeous face before me I'm starting to think that I wouldn't mind if our plan failed and I ended up with Alan instead. "He's jealous," whispers Alan, though that's plainly obvious, but I understand that Alan has to put a little emphasis on it. "We won't let him get away with that," I whisper back.

When the meeting is over, Alan and I leave hand in hand, very much to everyone's astonishment. We are literally passing through an alley of jaws dropped and mouths agape, a little hullabaloo roaring up as soon as we pass the door. He holds my hand partly to express our new "give-it-to-Leon" bond, but also because he is in a hurry to get to the sulky runaway, and he drags me along, pacing fast.

Well, I mentioned a "plan," but this was a bit of a euphemism. In fact, it isn't much of a plot, more of a one-component tactic: show him that he's not the only one who can play on other people's emotions, and then confront him.

We didn't even formulate a clearly defined aim, past "finding out the truth," which means much the same thing as "see what will happen and what comes out in the end." But I have the feeling that this is pretty much how far Alan's concept of a plan reaches in general. He's not the calculating sort.

Therefore, while we walk through the corridors und upstairs to Leon's room I try to sort out at least a few basics and whisper, "Listen, Alan, I want you to know I'm not in love with him, just in lust...so, I honestly wish you luck, and even though I'm badly in need of something to quench my desire...frankly, just the thought of you two getting it on will provide me with enough..."

"Shh...there's his door." He draws me closer, his eyes warm and kind. "Don't worry...I know what you're trying to say." For a moment, we lock eyes and it feels like we lock minds. We just smile and give each other an encouraging nod. Then his smile morphs into an eager snarl and the furrows on his forehead deepen beautifully with resoluteness as he turns to the door. "Shall we knock? I think not."

And we break in like a riot squad. Leon, who is sitting on the huge bed in the middle of the room drawing, flinches hard, sketch pad and pencil clattering to the floor. Judging from his expression, we must look like a monster and a vampire line-dancing through his nightmares.

With a laugh I jump on the bed and snuggle up to him, my hands instantly roaming all over him. Alan's still standing near the door. His palms rub over his jeans-clad thighs twice, like someone who's about to engage in really hard physical work, which makes me laugh even more.

One second later Alan's there. His hands rip off Leon's shirt in an instant, the harsh sound of the fabric being torn apart a loud sexy hiss. I watch Alan's tongue conquer Leon's mouth, forcing his lips open and pushing its way inside. The sounds are as arousing as the sight…the rustling rasp of Alan's stubble against Leon's, the little slurps and moans that escape their breathless kiss.

Any advantage from our surprise attack lasts about five seconds. Then I find my blouse gaping open and my breasts exposed, naked, before I even notice Leon's sneaky hand flipping the buttons, far too fascinated with the alpha male kiss in front of my eyes. Leon doesn't even interrupt the tongue-play with Alan or look at me once while he continues to undress me with his free hand, which gropes its way with an annoying practiced skillfulness and blind dexterity.

Still kissing Alan passionately with his eyes shut, he weighs one breast in his hand, then the other. I'm too transfixed in the evil hormonal spell to slap his insolent hand away. Then they finally need to breathe. Leon winks at me with this quirky crazy smirk of his, while—unbelievably—his left hand deftly opens Alan's jeans, slips inside and strokes Alan's cock to full hardness with a few, sure, knowing movements.

It's not the fact that he takes it up with both of us—after all, that's what we're here for—it's his record recovery time from bafflement, the speed and total self-assuredness with which he proceeds, and most of all his unerring determination that unsettles me. The man clearly knows he faces a challenge, and in no time has decided to win, taking the fast lane.

While I still try to catch up mentally, Alan starts to kiss me, which is not supporting my efforts to cling to my fast-slipping-away control. It is...I'm desperately scanning my brain for words, but there's an aphorism saying that as long as you notice details, you're not experiencing perfection, and Alan's kiss is exactly that. Completion. The kiss of kisses. The warmth and texture of his tongue, smoothness of his pliant lips; technique, masculine aggression combined with gentle consideration, all perfection. Within seconds I want to live inside his kiss, and it really feels as if the kiss is providing a cocoon of coziness all around me. Alan's body stiffens and shudders; it takes a moment before I figure out that Leon must have done something...and then suddenly Leon grabs both of our necks and breaks us apart, turning our heads just so, to compel our eyes upon him. He doesn't need much force, because again that comes too fast for us to build up physical resistance, but I can't believe the bastard dares to do this.

"Look at me," he demands, blatantly monopolizing our attention.

And then he simply goes for his intent. You will ask why we comply, why we don't stop him, and I think I have no other answer than: This is Leon. When he gets something into his head, it's near impossible to resist. I have watched him talking the whole cast and crew into things no one had the slightest inclination to do in the first place. Though "talking into" is not exactly the right expression; he doesn't use many words on these occasions. It's almost as if he imposes his purpose by sheer willpower, simply going through with what he wants and firmly expecting everyone to follow. His solid conviction that he will get his own way generates a sort of gravitation...you're just drawn to give in.

Similarly, he does without many orders now. He radiates them; with every movement and look, with every flick of his little finger, he calls the shots, he's in charge, on top, and in control. He arranges us like he wants us quietly and effectively, sometimes murmuring a few words to himself, concentrating on the erotic artwork he has in mind, obviously not expecting any serious resistance. In "bounce it, stretch it, tear it, mold it" manner he makes Alan kneel on all fours with his head bowed down and me straddling him facing backward, toward Leon, who kneels between Alan's legs, grabs Alan's hips, and lines up without any further ado.

I realize that Alan's already lubed—it must have been Leon's fingers in his ass that made him tremble while we kissed—but seeing the tip of Leon's huge cock point at that tiny pucker sends shivers through my nerves.

Leon makes sure I watch. He looks up through black strands of tousled hair with fiendish satisfaction, and he's so gorgeous like that I can't find it in me to disapprove of his possessiveness and thirst for power.

He pauses a moment to adjust my position, placing one hand on my shoulder and pushing a little downward, so that my weight presses down the small of Alan's back and he arches a little more. Very pleased, Leon checks whether my breasts are displayed at the right heights by giving them a test squeeze.

"Keep him still," Leon murmurs, and I get it that he wants me to pin Alan's waist between my legs, holding him fast. A moment later I also understand why this is necessary—Leon rams home with one decisive thrust, opening Alan up all the way, and Alan groans out loud beneath us. But he doesn't protest; I can hear the excitement and pleasure mixed with a little pain in his voice. That sound is so perfect that I'm moistening Alan's skin where my pussy rubs against it.

Leon rapidly accelerates his pounding, skin slapping on skin. My legs embrace Alan, making it impossible for him to move forward. He rides out Leon's harder thrusts, offering his ass to the assault.

Leon fucks Alan so hard his thrusts would have squashed him into the sheets if Leon hadn't used me like a living paperweight to force him to stay in his position.

As soon as Leon knows everything is in place according to his needs, he reaches out for my breasts, grasping them hard, one in each hand. A long gaze of fierce, intense pleasure, then his eyes shut and his head falls back, giving me a beautiful sight of his long sinewy neck and the dimple between his collarbones.

The bastard has created the ideal hermaphrodite hybrid for himself, a mysterious double-sexed creature—with ass and breasts conveniently accessible at the same time. Now he's shaking with lust—it's like pleasure is a demon that has obsessed him. When he opens his eyes again, thrusting deep into Alan's tight ass and clutching my pert flesh, his features transfigure with sexual bliss. Since when has selfishness become such a turn-on? I can't help myself; I've never seen anything more beautiful than Leon striving for his satisfaction.

His moves slow down a little; he rides Alan in sensual waves, his fingers flinch involuntarily while he still holds on to my breasts, and he leans forward to catch my mouth in a squelching kiss, still fucking Alan with long, strong thrusts. For a moment, I break the kiss and let my eyes wander down, down between my curvy, hairless body and the dusting of soft curls on Leon's front, down to where Leon's cock thrusts into the upturned ass. His cock is slightly tanned, while Alan's skin is very light. I can see every little detail like it's a close-up in a porn video, only I'm sure there's no porn as hot as watching how the thin skin of Alan's pucker stretches around Leon's cock.

I lift my eyes again, and Leon must be able to read, by the sheer dizziness and heat in them, what the sight does to me.

"Fuck him, Leon," I groan and kiss him again, pinching his nipples with my fingers. And Leon slams in Alan's ass, spilling his seed in spastic shudders, moaning his orgasm into my mouth.

I slide from Alan's back, slumping backward in order to rest against the headboard. Alan's head comes up, and I can tell by the gleam in his eyes and his amused smile he's enjoyed it. But neither he nor I have come yet. We both look at Leon, rightly expecting something of him.

But I wouldn't have dreamed that Leon—selfish bastard until a minute ago—would smile at us in genuine gratefulness and frankly say, "Thank you..." then lower his lashes and whisper, "I'm at your disposal now," completely changing his attitude.

Now that is too fast for me to adapt, but not for Alan, probably because he knows that Leon likes to play on both sides in every double meaning. My eyes go wide as Alan turns on the dominant mode and becomes all toppish.

Grasping a fistful of Leon's hair and wrapping it around his wrist with a flick and turn of his hand—it's long enough for that—he shoves Leon facedown between my legs. "Come on... do it...I know you like to go down."

And there's no doubt he does, because Leon opens his mouth wide, presses his tongue flat against my whole pussy, and then he swipes and licks and sucks as if he practiced for years, which

I bet he has. Oh, my god, who would have thought that Leon can eat pussy like that?

Alan's watching with glittering eyes, constantly licking his lips. Watching him lick his lips is nearly as hot as feeling Leon lick mine.

Alan slaps him hard. "Come on, slut…you can do better…give her as good as you give me…." I would have sworn such a thing was not possible, but Leon definitely tries even harder, drilling his tongue inside me, whirling, circling… I'm so wet, I'm soaked, positively drenched; Leon could very well drown in my come.

Alan prepares him now; I can see he knows very well what he's doing. There's the same calm, competent routine I noticed with Leon earlier, and suddenly I realize how much of a kick I get out of their supreme experience in and of itself…to watch these beautiful, sure hands doing what no doubt they've done countless times before, the clever, experienced hands of a man like Alan…

He slaps Leon again, primarily to get his attention or at least that's part of it—it's kind of an announcement that he's going to breach him—and Leon wiggles his ass in compliance. With a deep, rough sigh Alan starts to thrust. My position is even better now than while I watched Leon fuck Alan because I'm conveniently draped on the pillows, savoring Leon's attention while I enjoy the ultimate porn show right in front of my eyes.

Not to mention the soundtrack. Alan's panting heavily now, and if I was robbed of any other sensation than just Alan's desperate breathless panting literally pouring down my aural canal and stirring up each single hair on my skin, I'd still come from that.

Of course, Alan and I are both already close from before. Another slap, this time to indicate that he's about to come and Leon should speed up to get me off in time. Suddenly Leon does something that makes me feel as if he's balancing my lust and pleasure on the tip of his tongue. He keeps me on the edge for seconds, waiting for Alan, no doubt sensing when Alan will come by the way he moves inside him. He keeps almost still, only rocking softly against me from Alan's thrusts.

And then, right when I hear Alan crying out hoarsely, he uses a bit of a bite, scraping my clit with his teeth just the right way, sucking the flesh around it at the same time. A sharp sting of pleasure shoots up from the center of my lust between Leon's divine lips and roars through all my nerves and fibers, orgasm spreading like a wave of scalding heat, blowing up my brain in a blackout.

When my senses start to work again we're peacefully resting in the bed, Leon in the middle with an arm around each of us. Later still, the sex is gentle; they sandwich me, Leon entering my pussy and Alan taking me from behind. We drift along like a little cluster of pleasure floating on cloud nine.

After that we'd probably have simply fallen asleep if we weren't so thirsty. As it is, Leon gets up to fetch some water from the refrigerator. While we're sitting there guzzling it down I finally recall what this is all meant to be about. Apart from having had a more than entertaining time I'm not sure whether Alan and I have achieved anything on the "find the truth" track of action.

I start to dress and when Leon looks at me questioningly, I opt for a direct approach. "I think maybe you two should talk."

Following my example, Alan has already begun to pick up his clothes, too.

"Please...please, Alan, stay...she's right. Please..." Leon's really begging and I give Alan an encouraging smile, reassuring him it's okay with me.

And then I slip out the door, having got all I wanted and more, and wishing the same for Alan.

* * *

Three days later, and I haven't been able to talk to Alan yet because he and Leon are inseparable now, far too busy adoring each other with amorous glances and touches to interrupt.

Suddenly, commitment doesn't seem to be an issue for Leon anymore. I wonder merely out of curiosity why that is and what they talked about, because the outcome is what counts and it's just fine.

Like three days ago, as I'm drinking a beer at my usual place in the bar, looking over to where they sit and talk, smiling to myself.

After a while, they come over and ask whether I'd join them for a walk. Of course I'd love to, only outside a strong wind is howling and wheezing—a very strong wind. You can hear the gutters and shutters rattling and see the leaves tumbling along when you look outside the window. It's not a big surprise, though, that the fucking storm is exactly the reason why Leon wants to go for a walk now. With a sigh, I accept, not wanting to let the opportunity pass, but inwardly I'm grateful that it's Alan and not me who has to put up with Leon's craziness on a regular basis now.

We walk up a nearby hill—which of course gets us even more exposed to the storm. Soon Leon is a little ahead, impatiently forging ahead to the top, and I ask Alan—or rather, shout over the noise of the hurricane—what Leon wanted to tell him that night. It's not an ideal situation for such a conversation, but I can't hold it back. Luckily, the explanation for Leon's behavior is short: the more he realizes he's falling in love, the more he's afraid of becoming dependant. In effect, he flirts around more to make sure there will be some sort of backup and to indulge himself with the illusion of "all options open" even though his heart has long since closed the case.

To be honest, I know this dynamic all too well, so I don't find it difficult to understand. Only when Leon found that Alan could flirt around as well did his fear of losing him finally outweigh his obsession with autonomy.

We join Leon at the top. It's after sunset already, a faint shimmer of orange-violet-pink still lingering on the landscape and tainting our faces. "Come on…a little bit over here," calls out Leon; we have to fight against the wind to get there. Leon takes my hand and pulls me up, and I take Alan's. "Look…the wind's so strong here it can hold your weight…Give it a try…let yourself fall like this…."

Leon spreads his arms, holds his body stiff and simply throws himself forward, until he's hovering like he's in an antigravity chamber, at a forty-five-degree angle with only his toes touching the ground. Alan and I curse the crazy bastard, but now we're here, so there's no point in not trying. Then the three of us are leaning against the wind, hand in hand, falling and caught by a storm's embrace.

ABOUT THE AUTHORS

REBECCA BOYD is the pseudonym for a switchy, pervy writing student, though she's not anyone's faculty advisor and very rarely gives hand jobs. Her poetry has appeared in several small publications, and she is currently working on a novel.

LAYLA BRIAR is the freethinking alter ego (and best self) of an otherwise timid, overworked suburban hockey mom who makes a living as a writer/editor/researcher, who has actual nightmares about lack of school lunch ingredients, and who is secretly brilliant on RockBand.

Born in Virginia and later raised on a sailboat, **ANGELA CAPERTON** has traveled extensively and has grown up to appreciate the world in all its forms. Always looking for the next adventure, she continues to travel as fate permits and writes fantasy and erotica to keep her wanderlust in check. Currently she has three works available, *Inspiration,* an erotic novella set in Renaissance Florence, her erotic fantasy and 2008 EPPIE finalist, *Woman of the Mountain,* and her erotic fairy tale, *The Passions of Pearl.*

ELIZABETH COLVIN is a journalist with a dirty mind; she enjoys domination and submission almost as much as she loves shopping for shoes. She has been widely published in a variety of erotic collections and online outlets: she cautions strangers never to interrupt that quiet girl in the café corner with a MacBook Pro and Prada heels.

JANA CORELL is is the pseudonym of a Midwestern college student who is generally pretty mellow but occasionally dabbles in being a dominant bitch. "With A Smile on Your Face" is not exactly a true story, but she didn't really make all of it up, either.

B. J. FRANKLIN has five stories in print, the most recent being "Faith, Hope, and Chastity" in *Samhain Scorchers* by Whiskey Creek Press. Her other stories appear in anthologies edited by noted erotica editors such as Violet Blue, M. Christian, and Sage Vivant. She has also had several stories published on websites, including Goodvibes.com and Threepillows.com. She is a member of the Erotica Readers and Writers Association, is a Trekkie and, in her spare time, studies medicine at university. Visit her website at bj-franklin.com.

S. J. FROST resides on a mini-farm with many spoiled pets and a wonderfully understanding husband who humors her need to feed anything with fur, feathers, or scales. She graduated from the University of Toledo with a BA in English/creative writing. Her short stories have appeared in *Best Gay Romance 2007* (Cleis Press), *Ultimate Gay Erotica 2008,* and *Best Gay Love*

Stories: Summer Flings (Alyson Books), and in the soon to be released *Asian Spice*, the Eroticnoir.com anthology published by ATRIA/Simon and Schuster and edited by Zane.

ERICA K. is the pseudonym of a Midwestern advertising executive. This is her first published story.

MIRANDA LOGAN lives with her boyfriend, a hot genderqueer roommate or two, and several cats in Southern California, which is even more fun than it sounds. She is not quite a sexy librarian yet, but is working on it.

Writing is like oxygen, and sexuality is like chocolate frosting. **ANASTASIA MAVROMATIS**'s erotic stories have appeared on Good Vibes, Oysters and Chocolate, Tit-elation, and Scarlet Magazine. Her blog, Sexualite, was featured in Scarlet Magazine (Best of the Sex Blogs), and *Neos Kosmos Newspaper* (Melbourne). Anastasia Mavromatis resides in Sydney, Australia, where she publishes Lucrezia Magazine.

ANAIS MORTEN lives in Germany and works as a teacher of arts and physical education and as a guide for sports climbing. Her publishing experiences include various contributions in lesbian, gay, heterosexual, and queer anthologies and two novels published by Maennerschwarm Verlag in Germany.

ANUSHA RAMKISSOON-FORTE's erotic short fiction appears in various anthologies including *Best Women's Erotica 2008* and *Yes, Ma'am* from Cleis Press. Her stories have also been featured in several Black Lace *Wicked Words* collections.

REMITTANCE GIRL writes and lives in exile in Vietnam. She is a dedicated practitioner of online writing in all its forms and a cultivator of obscene orchids. She also lives at remittancegirl.com.

Canadian eroticist, environmentalist, and pastry-enthusiast **GISELLE RENARDE** is the author of *The Birthday Gift* (Dark Eden Press), short-story contributor to the upcoming *Mammoth Book of Erotic Confessions* (Constable & Robinson), *Love Bites* (Torquere Press), *Coming Together: With Pride, Coming Together: Out Loud* (Phaze), and poetry/erotica contributor to *The Longest Kiss: Women Write on Oral Sex* (Mojocastle Press). Online, Giselle has contributed erotic content to such websites as For the Girls and Hips and Curves. Ms. Renarde lives across from a park with two bilingual cats who sleep on her head.

TAMARA ROGERS is a widely published San Francisco–based slash writer under a variety of pseudonyms who resents that her Victorian disallows more than seven cats per apartment. A college dropout, she still fancies herself a postmodern philosophy geek who fetishizes dialectical conversation about the dominant role of Spock in his relationship to Kirk, and whether the isolating diaspora of the Federation ships led to the homoerotic fantasies enjoyed by many "Star Trek" slash writers.

MADDY STUART's writing has appeared in several anthologies including *Dirty Girls: Erotica for Women, Yes Sir: Erotic Stories of Female Submission, Sexist Soles: Erotic Stories about Feet and Shoes,* and *Secret Slaves: Erotic Stories of Bondage.* She lives in Toronto where she also dances, paints, and dabbles in various geekeries including improvisational theater and computer programming. She can be found at maddystuart.com.

VIRGIE TOVAR is a twenty-five-year-old San Francisco sexpert, breast activist, and author of the newly released erotic autobiography, *Destination DD: Adventures of a Breast Fetishist with 40DDs*. Virgie is a Bay Area native of Mexican and Iranian parentage. Virgie currently leads workshops in erotic self-discovery, bedroom enhancement, and erotic writing throughout the Bay Area. She is a certified sex educator through San Francisco Sex Information and works as a sex educator in the Mission district of San Francisco. Virgie has been featured on Women's Entertainment Television and Playboy Radio, and is a blogger for Box Magazine. Visit her on the web at BreastFetishist.com.

Born in the buckle of the Bible Belt, **AMY WADHAMS** rebeled at an early age. She is now attempting to make a living doing what she does best...thinking dirty. Her work has been published in *Best Women's Erotica 2008*.

SASKIA WALKER is a British author whose erotic fiction appears in more than fifty anthologies including *Best Women's Erotica, Hide and Seek, Secrets, The Mammoth Book of Best New Erotica, Stirring up a Storm,* and *Kink*. Her longer work includes the erotic novels *Along for the Ride, Double Dare,* and *Reckless*. Her website is saskiawalker.co.uk.

ABOUT THE EDITOR

VIOLET BLUE is the best-selling, award-winning author and editor of more than two dozen sexual health books and erotica collections, including e-books and audiobooks. Violet is the *San Francisco Chronicle*'s sex columnist and a *Forbes* Web Celeb. She is a professional sex educator, lecturer, podcaster, blogger, vlogger, porn/erotica reviewer, sex and technology futurist and expert, and well-known machine artist. She has written for outlets ranging from Forbes.com to *O, the Oprah Magazine*. Violet is also a fetish model, Laughing Squid guest blogger, GETV reporter, fun to follow on Twitter, and San Francisco native. Violet lectures about sexuality to cyberlaw classes at UC Berkeley (Boalt), tech conferences (ETech, SXSWi), sex crisis counselors at community teaching institutions (SFSI.org), and Google Tech Talks. Her podcast has been downloaded by millions and is notorious: "Open Source Sex" has been featured in *Wired, Newsweek* (MSNBC), and the *Wall Street Journal*. Wired named her one of the Faces of Innovation, and

Forbes calls her "omnipresent on the Web." Violet's tech site is Techyum.com; her multi-platform audio and e-books are at Digita Publications (digitapub.com); her popular website and blog is at tinynibbles.com.